I0736612

HOW TO CATCH A BODYGUARD

SPECIAL EDITION

CHESTER FALLS
BOOK THREE

ANA ASHLEY

Illustrated by
COVERS BY JULES

How to Catch a Bodyguard - Chester Falls Book 3
Original © 2020 by Ana Ashley
Special Paperback Edition: September 2023
ISBN-978-1-915031-07-5

How to Catch a Bodyguard is a work of fiction. Names, characters, businesses, places events and incidents are either products of the author's imagination or used in a fictitious manner. Any resemblance to actual persons, living or dead, or actual events is purely coincidental.

Cover design: Covers by Jules

Editor: Alphabitz Editing

Join Ana's Facebook Group *facebook.com/groups/CafeRoMMance* for exclusive content, and to learn more about her latest books at *anawritesmm.com*!

DEDICATION

This dedication was first printed in How to Catch a Prince.
Today it stands more correct than ever.

To everyone that has been on the other end of me moaning,
crying, despairing, laughing, hoping, working, dreaming.
To those close friends... cough... Rhys...cough...Beau... who have
been there for the above and more.
Your friendship and support means more than you'll ever know.

Ana

x

ABOUT HOW TO CATCH A BODYGUARD

When your life is in danger, the last thing you should do is fall in love...especially with your bodyguard.

Connor hasn't just had a bad day or bad week. More like a bad year. Things have been going downhill since his relationship ended, and to top it all off, his house has been ransacked.
Ever since James returned to Chester Falls a year ago, his past has come to haunt him. Especially in the image of his childhood best friend who ran out on him after a moment of weakness.
Two best friends reunited.
A bisexual awakening.
An escape artist pet turtle.
James's first and only instinct is to **protect** Connor from whoever is trying to harm him. But will being his **secret crush's bodyguard** end up putting his heart in harm's way?
Welcome to Chester Falls, where you can expect to meet sweet men, sexy situations, interfering friends, lots of feels, and a happy ever after.
Book Three in the Chester Falls series. How To Catch a Bodyguard is a sweet and steamy MM romance novel with no cliffhanger, and a guaranteed HEA.

JAMES

A year ago

$\mathcal{I}$'d always wondered what it would be like to see Connor Williams again. Would his bright green eyes still light up a room? Would he still have the same dusting of freckles over his nose and cheeks, so light that you almost couldn't see them unless you were too close? Would his shiny, copper-colored hair have turned a darker shade as he grew older?

It's not like I'd spent the last fifteen years thinking about him. Well, maybe a little. He was, after all, the first boy I fell for. What I hadn't expected was for the devastating feelings from the last time I'd seen him to come back in full force.

The way he'd looked into my eyes after I'd given him the first and most shattering kiss of my life. It had been so brief, it could barely be considered a kiss, and he hadn't pushed me away or hit me as I'd half expected.

No, he'd just stared at me looking confused. His eyes had become a dark forest green, and his lips were parted as if he wanted more. God, I'd so wanted more.

But instead, he just whispered, *"You kissed me."* And then he ran.

That same day, my mom told me we were moving, and I never had a chance to talk to Connor again. To say goodbye, to apologize.

Now, staring into those same green eyes, at the same copper-colored hair, I was that fifteen-year-old boy again. The one who had never understood why two such different kids became friends to start with, other than it just had been that way.

Connor had been the popular kid. He'd played football and had had the whole boy-next-door look going for him. I bet he'd even mowed the lawn for his neighbors and delivered newspapers on the weekend.

I'd mostly spent my time at home in the small two-bedroom house I'd shared with my mom in Bethany, a few miles outside of Chester Falls. I'd been skinny and awkward and hadn't understood why the most beautiful boy at school had wanted to be my friend.

The difference between now and then was that, amongst other things, I'd grown into my body. I was no longer the gangly, fifteen-year-old boy Connor had known. And I certainly wasn't the same naive kid that had misunderstood his friend's closeness for attraction.

Warmth rushed through my body as Connor's eyes locked with mine. His brows furrowed, creating a cute V on his forehead. My fingers twitched, wanting things they had no place wanting, such as smoothing out that little crinkle above Connor's nose.

"But first, let me introduce you to Captain James Bennett."

The voice of my friend Kris, the Prince of Lydovia, brought me back into the reason for being here.

"James is my protection detail while I'm in America," Kris carried on as he revealed his identity to his boyfriend Charlie's family. Well, fake boyfriend.

Somehow, since I'd dropped Kris off in Chester Falls, he'd gone and fallen for the gentle Charlie after deciding to stand in as Charlie's boyfriend at his sister Hannah's wedding to her girlfriend, Ellie.

I'd never met Connor's family, and with Charlie having bright red hair, it never occurred to me that they would be related, even though they shared a surname. It was clear now, seeing them in the same room, that they were brothers. Same green eyes, same nose, same freckles.

As a bodyguard, my job was to protect those under my charge, but I'd also been hired for this particular job because I was a friend, and with my Special Ops background, I had the relevant experience, which meant I wasn't just hired muscle.

In fact, what most people aside from Kris didn't know was that my muscle was mainly for show. Yes, I could use my size and my strength in a fight, and I had pretty good aim with a gun, but I didn't like to use either. My strength came from intuition, observation, and analysis before the need for action.

Finding out Connor was Charlie's brother was like a sucker punch to the stomach. My brain worked hard to think of any clues I'd missed, because as Kris and Charlie discussed the ramifications of a press leak, all I could think was what was Connor's role in the whole thing, considering the journalist making the threat was his girlfriend.

Even though my eyes had been looking straight ahead, I'd been keeping an eye on everyone in the family for their reaction. And then, because I was a sucker for punishment, I looked at Connor again.

I couldn't read him, but there was no mistaking the tension in his frame. His forearms were resting on his knees while his hands were fisted in a way I bet caused his nails to dig into his palms, and his gaze remained fixed on the carpeted floor.

Suddenly, he stood up and walked toward the door, but I stepped in his way. He hadn't expected the move because he'd stopped still, mere inches from me. So close, I could feel the warmth from his body through his shirt.

I crossed my arms to give us some distance and make myself look taller, bigger, and stronger. I'd always been just that little bit taller than Connor, but it had never been noticeable as kids because he'd always been bigger thanks to his football training.

It was a dick move, but I couldn't be sure that he wouldn't leave the room to share Kris and Charlie's plans with his girlfriend.

Even though I was six foot ten, Connor was only an inch shorter than me, so it didn't take much for our eyes to meet again.

When they did, it was as though everyone in the room vanished and there was only Connor and I. Two fifteen-year-old friends waiting for the bus while sharing a bag of Skittles and fighting over who got to eat the red ones.

Connor's green eyes were bright, but he also looked exhausted. I don't know how long we stood there staring at each other, but it was long enough for me to revisit the little pattern of freckles under his eyes that looked like star constellations.

I'd always used to joke with him that I could read the horoscope on his face and made up ridiculous predictions based on them. Connor had hated his freckles. He'd said they made him look like a girl, but I'd thought they were perfect, even though I'd never dared say it out loud.

I knew the moment he'd finally recognized me because his eyes opened wider and he took half a step back, his mouth parting slightly and a small breath escaping from between his lips.

Connor looked at the people in the room as though, just like me, he'd only just remembered they were there.

"James," Kris called. "Let him go."

"Kris, you don't know—"

He held his hand up so I had no choice but to follow orders and let Connor leave the room.

I hoped Kris's trust in Connor wasn't misplaced because I

wasn't so sure, especially when, not thirty minutes later, a knock on the door announced the arrival of Connor and his girlfriend, Ceecee Bloomfield, the journalist who was trying to leak both Kris's location and Charlie's identity to the general public.

What followed was the kind of crisis management and planning I'd only ever seen before a deployment.

The Williams family had rallied around Kris and Charlie like a protective shield of love. It was clear to everyone that Kris and Charlie had fallen head over heels for each other, even if the family didn't know the whole thing had started off as fake.

Twenty-four hours later, not only had I been proven wrong about Connor, but I'd seen his loyalty to his brother and his family in the way he'd put his own heartbreak aside to support them.

Ceecee had come through on her promise to keep the story out of the press until the end of the wedding, but I still didn't trust her. So, despite Charlie's mom's kind invite to join the wedding party, I wasn't ready to face Connor again.

Sticking to checking the perimeter of the hotel in order to avoid bumping into Connor didn't do me any good when I turned a corner around a tall hedge in the garden and nearly bumped into him.

"Watch where—" He stopped as soon as he saw it was me.

I stood there not knowing what to say, but when the silence between us became too heavy to handle, I simply said, "Hi."

"Hi," he said.

More silence. I hated silence.

"Connor," I said, even though I didn't know what would follow next.

"Nice to see you again, James," Connor said as he walked off.

The last time he'd done it, I'd wanted to chase after him. This time, I knew not doing it was for the best.

My body's reaction to seeing him, despite everything, told me my heart wasn't safe around Connor.

"Goodbye, Con," I whispered to myself as if the statement would bear more weight if it was out in the world.

It didn't matter anyway. My last deployment would start as soon as Kris was back in Lydovia, and then it was anyone's guess as to where in the world I'd end up.

CONNOR

I scrunched up my nose and tried to look through the waterfall.

Yup, there were at least two rainbows, or maybe there were three? Dammit, the third one disappeared.

Ah well, such is life, I thought. We lose things all the time. Our safety net. Our sanity.

One moment it's there, and the next everything is gone, just like that rainbow.

I uncrossed my eyes so all I saw was the water cascading down from the top of the rocks all the way down to the river.

I took another swig of my beer, but the bottle was empty. What the fuck?

"Nevermind," I muttered to myself, the sound of my voice drowned under the noise of the waterfall. "There are plenty more where that one came from." I was sitting on an uneven rock, so when I reached for the pack of beers, I lost my balance and ended up on the hard stone ground. I laid back, feeling the cold rock beneath me, my gaze focused on the ceiling.

A laugh rose up from my belly, sounding louder than I expected and echoing around the empty walls of the cave, coming back as if it was mocking me.

The sound rang in my ears until it was no longer laughter. My vision was blurred, and tears ran down the sides of my face.

I tried to clean them with the sleeve of my shirt, but they just kept coming.

How had I got here?

Twelve months ago, I had everything. The career, the relationship, the life I'd worked so hard to make for myself.

I'd just been promoted, was earning the kind of money I'd only dreamed of, and my job as an HR project manager for one of the biggest construction companies in New Haven was interesting and challenging. I loved it.

My girlfriend, Ceecee, had decided we should move in together, so we were going to. It felt like a natural progression in our relationship.

I'd assumed we'd eventually get married, have kids, and maybe move back to Chester Falls, where my parents would help us look after them.

Then, almost overnight, everything went to shit, and here I was now. Single and doubting every one of the career decisions I'd made in my life. I was simply the guy whose job was to hire and fire, and fuck if I didn't hate the firing part.

I sat up and leaned against the rock I'd been using as a seat, stretching my legs out.

Below the hem of my trousers, I saw the design of my happy socks with footballs. A present from Charlie on the day he announced his move to Lydovia to be with Kris.

We'd all been at our parents' house. It was a hot summer's day, and as usual, my dad was at war with the grill and Uncle John was supervising to make sure no one got food poisoning. My sister Hannah and her wife Ellie were on salad duty and arguing over their all-time favorite romance novels while mom was making apple cobbler, the scent of fruit and cinnamon wafting through the entire house.

Charlie and Kris came out from Charlie's room to join the rest of the family. Kris squeezed my shoulder as he walked past where I was sitting at the top of the stairs. I expected Charlie to follow, but he sat down next to me.

"Do you remember when we used to sit up here on Christmas Eve waiting for Santa to come?" Charlie had said.

"We thought we were so smart." I shook my head at how ingenious we were.

"And we always woke up in bed the next morning thinking Santa had tucked us in."

I'd chuckled. "Quite a creepy thought when you think of it now."

He'd laughed and bumped my shoulder with his.

"Con, are you okay?" Charlie asked.

"Yeah, go on and rescue Kris. I'm sure I heard Aunt Gina saying something about cocktails earlier, and I wouldn't put it past her to lace his with something strong so she can have her way with him."

Charlie didn't call me out on my clear lie, but he did join Kris in the kitchen where he'd been roped into cutting fruit for Gina's deadly drinks.

I hadn't been okay at that moment.

I'd watched my loving family as if I was an outsider. They loved me, but I didn't feel I belonged because I didn't trust myself anymore, and I'd lost who I thought I was.

Everyone around looked like they had their shit together. Hannah was married, Charlie was now engaged, and to a prince no less, while I was just... flailing.

I looked at the stone ceiling of the cave and the naturally occurring patterns of the rocks.

Charlie and I had discovered this cave years ago. It was nested on the hill, and it was so close to the waterfalls that if you stood right on the edge of the cave, you could feel a spray of water.

The cave was too high up to have access to the water, but the magic of it was in the view and the fact it was a special place that no one else knew about.

I'd only brought one person here, and I didn't want to think about that. And as far as I knew, Charlie had only ever brought Kris here.

I dragged myself over to the pile of blankets Charlie and I had stolen from my parents to find they'd been replaced with nicer, plusher ones, and lots of them.

Maybe Charlie had brought them last time they were home. It had been a while since I'd had time to come to the cave.

Tiredness came over me. Despite the warm summer temperatures, inside the cave, it was always much cooler. I picked a few of the blankets and lined them up before I lay on top of them. These were definitely nicer than the old, ratty ones we had. I should be happy, but instead, I felt sad that this was one more thing that was different, had been replaced with better.

My eyes were heavy, so I allowed the buzz from the alcohol to settle in my stomach and send me off to sleep.

The sound of a deep, calm voice threatened to wake me from my slumber. I wished it away even though the sound of it soothed something inside me.

"I found him. I'm going to stay with him... yeah... Ryan should be okay, but call me if you need me... okay."

I relented and opened my eyes.

Jamie Fucking Bennet was crouching down next to me. No, he wasn't Jamie anymore. He'd lost the privilege to be Jamie when he left me without any warning or a goodbye.

I rubbed my eyes and sat up, leaning against the cave wall, shivering as the cold suddenly hit me.

James picked one of the blankets and put it around me. He smelled of fresh shower soap with only a hint of cologne.

I shook my head to clear my thoughts. What the fuck was I doing thinking about how clean he smelled?

"What are you doing here?" I asked.

His eyes were trained on me as if he was unsure how to answer the question. I gestured at him to let him know I was waiting for a reply and not happy about him invading my secret space.

His lack of an answer was maddening, adding to the pounding in my head.

I reached out for the pack of beers and took another one, unscrewing the top and taking a swig. If he was going to stand there looking all tough, that was fine with me as long as he carried on being silent. I had come here to get drunk, and despite my short nap, I was still on target to achieve my goal.

He reached for my bottle, but I was too quick for him, yanking it away from him. "Hey," I snapped.

If my reflexes were still good, then I wasn't drunk enough. Yet.

James sat next to me and reached for the blanket that had ridden down my back.

"This is my spot," I said. "You're not allowed here anymore."

I heard him exhale, but he still didn't say anything, and because the beer and lack of food were finally getting to my head, I kept talking.

"I waited every single day for a month. Did you know that?" I shook my head. "No, I don't suppose you do." I took another swig of the beer because I needed to stop talking before I admitted to my former best friend that I'd been completely devastated when he hadn't turned up for school the day after that kiss. And then heartbroken when, day after day, I'd waited at his bus stop before going to school and he was never among the people getting off.

"What are you doing here, James? Aren't you supposed to be with my brother and Kris?"

"They have another bodyguard with them."

"So what, you're bodyguarding *me* now?" I started laughing. I didn't know why I found that funny, but I couldn't stop.

I looked at James, and there was a hint of a smile on his lips, and a small dimple appeared on his right cheek. I remembered that dimple.

Suddenly, the atmosphere around me seemed to crackle. My mouth felt dry and my hands were damp.

"Con, we need to go," he said, his voice gentle despite the lines on his forehead.

"What?"

"We need to go," he repeated with a little less patience.

"No, you called me—"

"Connor, we need to leave. *Now*," he said, getting up.

His commanding voice was back. Fuck if I was going to be told what to do by the sack of muscles.

"No, *you* can go. This is still my spot, and I'm staying," I said crossing my arms.

"Fuck, Connor, just do what you're told for once," he shouted.

Okay, now he *was* angry.

I got up, ready to give him a piece of my mind, but instead, I stumbled as I tried to hold myself up by using the wall of the cave.

"Jesus, Connor," he shouted as he pulled me back from the rocky edge. I hadn't realized how close I'd come to falling over.

My heart was beating out of my chest as I struggled to draw a breath. I sat on the stone rock and put my hands on my knees, those pesky tears threatening to come back.

"Please, Connor." There was a pleading tone to his voice that was different from before.

I hated that my will to follow James was stronger than the will to defy him, so I didn't say anything. A nod of my head would have to be enough.

JAMES

How was it possible to want to kill someone while also wanting to wrap them in cotton wool?

I'd been in several war zones. I'd saved countless lives and also killed more than I wanted to remember. Being able to predict and control my environment was something I'd worked hard for and had been fairly successful at until now.

Connor, my former childhood best friend, somehow had the ability to take all that away, and more, he also made me feel helpless. That was not something I wanted to feel ever again, which in turn made me angry at him.

"Connor," I said, trying to contain my frustration.

It hadn't even been twenty-four hours since I'd arrived back in Chester Falls, and I was already wondering if taking up Kris's offer to be his head of security had been a bad idea.

The snow-capped mountains and the green forests of Lydovia had been my refuge the last three months since my final deployment, but I'd known at some point, Kris and Charlie would want to visit Charlie's family.

I knew that accepting the job as Kris's head of security meant I would eventually bump into Connor again, but knowing and being ready for it were two different things. And now, here I was, trying to convince the man to leave his cave so I could make sure he was safe.

Seeing him trip so perilously close to the edge nearly took my sanity away. I thought he was going to be sick after I pulled him back into a safer spot in the cave, but he stood there silently. It was a full minute until he stood up and nodded.

I stretched my hand out to support him so he wouldn't trip on the way out of the cave, but he didn't take it.

"Fine." My nerves were already frayed, so I turned my back on him and walked back toward the path. He could follow me or not. I didn't give a shit.

"Why did you leave?" I heard Connor ask behind me.

The path was overgrown, so I used my focus to push all the tree branches aside as an excuse to avoid answering the question.

"Fuck," Connor said.

I turned around to find him attempting to untangle his jacket from a thorny bush. He waved his arms around and finally became free just in time to trip over a small rock and fall ass first on the path. Thank fuck we'd walked far away enough from the waterfall.

"Need help?" I asked.

"No," he grunted. "And you can wipe the smirk off your face, jackass."

"I'm the jackass? You're the one getting stuck in a bush, tripping over yourself, and refusing any kind of help."

This time he took the hand I reached out to help him get on his feet.

As soon as he was up, he stepped around me and resumed the walk up the path toward the gate with the *Private Property* sign he'd put up years ago.

I followed him until he stopped short of the gate.

"What's wrong?" I asked.

Connor turned around and stared at me. I looked behind to see if there was something wrong, but there was nothing but tree branches, bushes, and overgrown weeds that now hid the path we'd just walked on.

He seemed to struggle with whatever was going on inside his head, but then he moved into my space and put his arms around me. I wasn't expecting it, so I stiffened at the unexpected hug, but as soon as I felt Connor try to withdraw, I tightened my arms around him.

"You're not okay, Con," I said. He didn't know the reason I'd come for him, so I suspected he was already something in his mind.

"Ice cream," he replied, and my mind went back to the day we'd come up with the code word.

"I hate biology," Connor said, closing the study book, leaning back in his chair and stretching his arms behind his back.

I looked around and, sure enough, Mrs. Green, the librarian, was staring at us. He'd spoken just a little louder than the micro whisper she allowed.

Ms. Hill was less strict, so when we saw she wasn't in the library today, we almost went straight back out, but we had a test coming up.

"Why do you hate biology?" I asked, already knowing what his answer was going to be.

"Because it's stupid."

Whenever Connor didn't have an answer for something, he always said the same thing. He didn't mean it, really. He was just the kind of person who preferred to be outside than with his nose in a book.

"Biology is the study of life and how living and nonliving organisms interact with each other," I said and then leaned over the table toward him. "From the looks you were giving Stacey in class earlier, I'd say you're very much into biology."

I chuckled before a paper airplane hit me right on the forehead.

Then Mrs. Green coughed, causing me to look over toward her, and she pointed toward the door.

"Come on, let's go before we get kicked out," I said.

Connor's smile was as bright as the sunshine outside the library. We ran down the stairs outside until we were both out of breath and laughing our heads off.

"I thought Mrs. Green was going to have a stroke when you knocked over that chair," he said, doubling over in laughter.

"I know, right!"

"I think we should can biology and go have some ice cream," Connor said, pointing at the ice cream truck parked by the town square.

It took us a ridiculous amount of time to pick our ice cream flavors before we sat on a bench in the square.

"I can't believe after all that you went with vanilla," he said, shaking his head. My eyes zeroed on the movement of his Adam's apple as he licked his peanut butter and chocolate ice cream.

"Vanilla is the best flavor. You can dress it up, and it will never let you down."

Connor looked at me with his big green eyes, but I looked away and focused on my own ice cream. Sometimes when he looked at me like that, I didn't know what was going on in his head.

"So...biology," he said, bumping his knee against mine. "Anyone in class you want to get biologically close to?"

"Seriously, dude?"

He laughed. "Oh, come on. Mandy totally digs you."

"Ice cream," I said, taking the final bite of my wafer cone.

"What?"

"I love ice cream. We should have it every day forever."

He laughed louder, and the sound reached that part inside me where all my secrets were kept, including how Connor's smile made me feel.

"Fine, dude, don't tell me about Mandy."

From that day on, every time there was something we didn't want to talk about, we always used *ice cream* as our code word. Granted, I'd used it a lot more than Connor had, mostly because my biggest secret was something I was too terrified to talk about.

"Let's go. It's cold out here," I said. A cool breeze had picked up this afternoon, and while it wasn't totally unpleasant, it had to feel cool for Connor with his damp clothes.

Connor nodded and gave me one final squeeze before he let go and resumed the walk.

"Will you tell me what happened?" he asked.

"What do you mean?"

"After that day. I never saw you again. Was it because of me?"

I hated the insecurity in his voice. Did he think I'd left because he'd rejected me?

My mom's decision had turned my life upside down, and at fifteen, I'd just been angry and hurt. Angry with my mom and hurt that Connor had run after the kiss without letting me apologize for the misunderstanding, but I never saw it from his point of view.

We walked through the old gate and up another path toward the Falls parking lot where I'd seen his car earlier. I'd parked mine next to his.

When he tried to unlock his car, I turned him around and pressed him against the door.

"First of all, you're not driving. You're still drunk," I said.

His jaw ticked, and his eyes were defiant. He wasn't going to make it easy for me.

"I was fifteen, Connor," I sighed. "It... it wasn't because of you."

"Then why?"

"Ice cream," I said using our code word.

He tilted his head and smiled.

"Come on, let's get inside my car. It's cold, and we need to talk."

"About what?"

"The reason you missed Tom's store pre-opening party and went missing, leaving everyone worried about you."

He rubbed his eyes. "What are you talking about? Tom's party is tomorrow."

"No, Connor, it was today."

"Fuck." He groaned.

CONNOR

I took my phone out of my pocket, but it was dead. I couldn't believe I'd missed Tom's party.

When Tom moved to Chester Falls from Boston, my brother Charlie had asked me to keep an eye on his sparklier-than-life best friend.

It was my fault that we weren't closer as friends, but I did love Tom, and I was really proud of what he'd achieved. After working so hard to open his fashion store, Fabulize, Tom deserved all the support he could get, and I couldn't help but feel I'd let him down by not being there for him on such a special day.

"What time is it? I can still make it. Or at least I'll go and apologize to him. If you won't let me drive, please give me a lift there," I pleaded as I went around the car to the passenger side and got in.

James turned the car on, but instead of driving us away, he handed me a small bottle of water he took out of a bag in the backseat.

"What's going on? Why aren't we moving?" I asked. Had something happened? Was he trying to sober me up so he could deliver bad news?

"Oh my god, is everything okay with Charlie?" I sat motionless in my seat, the bottle stopped halfway to my lips.

"Yes, Charlie is fine, and so is Kris and everyone else."

James turned in his seat to face me. He looked concerned, which was confusing since he'd just told me Charlie and Kris were okay. I knew they'd traveled from Lydovia to attend Tom's party, which I guessed was also the reason James was around.

"Then what? You're worrying me."

"Did you know your house was broken into?"

I laughed, and because I didn't know any other way to react to such ridiculous news, I laughed some more.

"Connor?"

"Sorry," I said, trying to get my breathing back. "It's just that with all the shit in my life, if you told me my house had fallen into the Chester River, I still wouldn't be surprised, and I don't even live anywhere near the river."

"This is how it's going to go," James said as he put his hand on the arm I had resting on the console between us. "We're taking you home so we can assess for any damage and figure out what's missing, then I'm taking you to my place until we know if this is a random event or if you're being targeted."

I hated taking shit from people, especially since I already spent so much of my life being told what to do, but there was something in James's voice I couldn't read, so I fastened the seat belt around me.

It didn't mean I'd agreed to his plan, but I was tired, still slightly drunk, and now I had to assess my home after a potential break-in. Fuck my life.

Fortunately, the drive to my place wouldn't take long, so I didn't feel the need to make small talk.

Unfortunately, my brain decided it was a good time to revisit the hug I'd forced on him earlier. Fuck if I could make any sense of my behavior, but it had felt really good to take a moment of comfort when I'd been feeling so vulnerable.

I hadn't seen James since my sister's wedding a year ago, and while I'd often thought about how he'd suddenly appeared back in my life, I hadn't had the guts to ask Charlie about Kris's bodyguard.

Well, he hadn't actually appeared in my life, he'd just appeared, and, like before, he'd just as quickly disappeared.

Charlie and Kris had visited a few times, but they always had a different bodyguard with them, a guy named Ryan who looked friendly and deadly in equal measure.

"So, you're James Bennet now?" I asked.

"Yeah."

"What happened to Lexington?"

He kept his eyes on the road, but I didn't miss the tick of his jaw as he answered with a nondescript grunt.

"The James I knew used to be a lot chattier," I teased. "Back in the day, no one could shut you up."

"The James you knew doesn't exist anymore."

I didn't believe that for one second. The concern in his eyes as I woke up in the cave told me as much, but I didn't call it out.

There was a police car parked outside my house when we arrived.

I made a move to get out of the car as soon as we parked, but James stopped me by putting his hand on my arm again. It felt warm and strong.

"What," I said.

"Let me take the lead."

"Why?" I asked.

"The brother of the fiance of the Prince of Lydovia had his house broken into. It could be nothing, or it could be a security risk. This is my job, so let me do it."

"Fine," I said, louder than I'd intended. If I was just a job, then he could do whatever the hell he needed to do and then leave.

I got out of the car and greeted the police officer halfway to my house.

"Mr. Williams, I'm officer Scott LaCruz," he said, holding out his hand.

"Please, call me Connor," I said, shaking his hand.

I hadn't taken my hand back yet when I felt James's presence behind me. A shiver ran up my spine, but I wasn't sure if it was because of James's assertive presence or the cold that had seeped through my damp clothes.

"Connor, we had a call about a disturbance at this address. When I drove past, I saw the door open, but I didn't see a car in the driveway, so I parked to check everything was okay. When I knocked and called out and there was no reply, I went in."

"Officer LaCruz, I'm Captain James Bennett. Can you tell me everything you know?"

Officer LaCruz nodded and started walking toward my front door.

"Wait." I held my hands up to stop them. I had questions that needed answering, and it was pissing me off that James was taking over. "James, how did you know my house was broken into, and officer, how did you know my name?"

"Please, call me Scott. Your sister volunteers at the police station when we have situations involving minors and family disputes. I've dropped her here once when we finished a shift together, so I recognized the address," Scott said.

"Hannah was in Bookmarked when she got the call from Scott. Everyone was worried because they hadn't seen you and you weren't answering your phone. That's when I went looking for you," James said.

Everything was slowly slotting into place. Well, everything apart from the break-in.

"Okay, am I allowed inside?" I asked.

Scott gave me a set of keys. Apparently, while there was no damage to the door, the lock had needed changing. It wasn't exactly his job to babysit a house, but it seemed he'd done it for Hannah while Charlie had organized the locksmith.

My hands shook as I put the key in the lock to open the door. James, who hadn't put more than two feet between us since we'd left the car, put his hand on my shoulder.

His presence was reassuring. God, I was getting whiplash from my seesaw of feelings about James, because I was both glad he was here and annoyed by his presence.

"Oh my god." I gasped. Nothing had prepared me for the utter destruction I saw as soon as I opened the door.

All the pictures I had hung up in the hallway were on the floor. There was glass everywhere, and I could see a couple of my favorite childhood photos were completely ruined.

I knelt down to pick them up, tears stinging at the back of my eyes.

"Connor, can you tell me if there's anything that stands out to you?"

Scott's voice caught my attention. I nodded and stood up.

Each room I went in was a mess. Drawers pulled out, clothes everywhere. Anything that previously hung on a wall was now scattered on the floor, most things broken beyond repair.

All the cupboards in the kitchen were open, too, and some of the dishes were smashed. I went straight for the place I'd kept my favorite cup and let out a sigh of relief when I found it intact.

"Is that the one we got on that school trip to Boston?" James asked.

"Yes."

It had been a silly thing to buy since I was into football, James hadn't been into sports at all, and neither of us drank coffee at the time. He'd said it was the reason we couldn't not buy them, and so we did.

Sixteen years later, the Red Sox cup was still my favorite, and even though it always lived at the back of the cupboard, it was always the one I reached for whenever I was having a particularly bad day.

Lost in my memories, I barely noticed James and Scott discussing the break-in. That was when I ran to the living room, not caring about any of the glass under my shoes.

My heart sank at the sight of the mess on the floor.

"Nooo!" I screamed.

JAMES

My heart broke for Connor as much as my protective nature was crying out for action.

Even though Scott had said he'd already cleared the house and there was no one in it, I still felt the need to check each room.

Connor's house was all on one level, which made it easier to check, but it also presented an aspect of vulnerability if whoever destroyed his house came back for more.

Because that's what they'd done, they'd destroyed it. There wasn't a single piece of furniture in place, drawer unopened, knick knack untouched.

Scott went around each room with me, agreeing something didn't feel right about this break-in.

"Nothing seems to be missing," he said. "It's like someone came in with the intent of turning the house inside out."

"Could they be looking for something specific?" I asked.

"Possibly, but only Connor will be able to tell."

We walked back to where Connor was staring outside the window with the Red Sox cup still in his hand.

The only way to explain the look in his eyes ever since I'd seen him for the first time last year was haunted, lost, and even though he was facing away right now, I knew what I'd see if he looked back at me.

Scott gestured toward the front door, and I followed him.

"James, I need to go back and file the report. Can you call me if Connor finds anything odd or out of place?" He handed me his card and then sighed. "I mean more out of place."

"I will."

"When Connor is ready, tell him to stop by the station so I can take a statement from him and give him a copy of the report for his insurance."

Scott was already halfway up to his car when I said, "Scott, I haven't lived in Chester Falls for a long time. Is this kind of break-in usual?"

"No more than in any other town or city across the country, but I'd stay with him for a while just in case. He looks like he'll need a friendly face around."

I nodded and looked back toward the house. A friendly face. We'd been friends before, so maybe it was time to get over the past and get to know this older, less self-assured Connor.

A scream got me removing my gun from the holster and running back to the house.

"Connor!" I shouted.

I found him in the living room. He was on his knees on the floor, his hands over his face, and he was sobbing. I was careful to go around the glass that was spread all over underfoot.

It was as I got closer that I noticed the floor was wet.

"What happened?"

"She's not here, James," Connor cried.

"Who?"

Instead of answering my question, he looked at me like he'd remembered something.

"She's gone," he said. "James, maybe she escaped. She's good at that. Help me look for her."

He started looking around the room, under the furniture,

behind the curtains. It was like his ass was on fire as he moved around.

"Tell me what you're looking for so I can help you," I said, frustration rising in my chest as I holstered my gun.

We needed to do a proper search of the house for whatever it was the thieves wanted, and I needed to do it with Connor.

"Bubbles, I'm looking for Bubbles," he said, getting past me toward his room.

"What the fuck is a Bubbles?"

"My pet. She escapes sometimes, so maybe they didn't get to her."

I could tell he said it in the hope that it would be true.

"I didn't see a cat or dog when I checked all the rooms. Is Bubbles a pedigree? Would they have wanted her to sell?"

Connor looked at me and shook his head like I was being stupid. I remembered the set up in the living room. It looked like a water tank had been smashed.

"Fuck, please tell me your pet isn't a baby anaconda."

"Of course not. It's a turtle."

I took a sigh of relief. A turtle I could handle. He was searching under his bed, moving everything around.

When he stood up, I put my hands on his shoulders. "What does Bubbles look like?" I asked.

"She's a yellow-bellied slider, so she has yellow and green stripes, and her belly is yellow too. She's only three inches long."

"You said she escapes sometimes. Where does she normally go?"

He shouted "the backyard" as he released himself from my hold and moved out of the living room.

I followed him but stopped in my tracks when I saw most of his backyard was grass and we were looking for the tiniest pet in the world. There was a decked area just outside the back door, so I joined Connor.

How the hell had she got out?

"She's normally easy to spot because of her color, but it's getting dark, so we need to be careful."

Connor stepped carefully onto the grass, and I had to close my eyes. There was no way I'd follow. I didn't want to be responsible for the demise of the little creature that seemed to mean so much to him.

I got on my knees to see the grass at an angle that would hopefully make it easier to spot anything moving on it. A little rustling noise over by the wooden step caught my attention.

I smiled as I saw the tiny little thing struggle to get herself in an upright position.

"Hello, sweetheart. You've made your daddy worried sick," I said to her before I picked her up and placed her on my palm.

"I've got her, Connor."

As I got up to turn toward Connor, the little hellion bit my finger.

"Fuck! Shit."

"Oh my god, Bubbles!" Connor cried. "Oh god, thank you. Thank you." He put his hands under mine to coax her to release my finger and amble back to his hand.

"Aww, come here, Sweet Pea," he cooed. "You must be so scared. That's okay, I'm here now, and I promise the big man isn't that scary."

My finger was throbbing from the bite, but I'd take the pain any day to see Connor smile again the way he did when his eyes set on the tiny creature.

"The big man needs all of his fingers," I said, giving the tiny turtle a pointed stare, not that she looked bothered or repentant.

It was only then I realized how mine and Connor's heads were so close together and our hands were still touching as we made sure Bubbles was okay.

I looked up. Connor's bright green eyes were on me. His smile, so familiar as if he hadn't grown into an adult over the last fifteen years. A very good looking adult at that.

Fuck.

I took a step back to get some distance but tripped on the decked steps and ended up on my ass in the grass.

"Thank fuck we found the turtle already," I said.

Connor opened his mouth like he was going to say something, but then he just started laughing.

I propped myself up with my elbows and tried to look hurt, but I couldn't help laughing with him.

"Shall we give Mr. Muscle a hand up? What do you think, Bubbles?" he said, turning to the tiny turtle and scratching her head. The little devil closed her eyes, relishing the touch.

"Mr. Muscle? Like you can talk, Thor." I smiled at the use of the silly nickname because Connor wasn't much smaller than me. He'd always been athletic, thanks to all the hours of training he endured, so it wasn't surprising that he still looked as strong as an adult.

What caught me off guard was how firm but gentle his hand was as he pulled me up from the grass while still holding Bubbles with the other hand.

I couldn't help imagining how his touch would feel as he pinned me against a wall and took me from behind, showing me exactly how he could control my pleasure.

My dick hardened in my dress trousers. Thank god I'd been on duty when Connor had disappeared because my jeans wouldn't have been as forgiving when it came to showing where my mind had taken me.

The reminder of how I'd found Connor and all of the day's events was enough to deflate my erection and get me back to what I did best.

"Connor, I need you to go around the house and tell me if you think anything has been taken. Then, we're going to stop by the pet store and get Princess Bubbles a new, temporary home. You're coming to stay with me at the Old Mill apartments."

I went back into the house without looking back. If Connor

challenged me on this, I wasn't sure how I would handle it. Something was up with him and this break-in situation, and the need to get him out into a safe place until I could figure things out was stronger than anything I'd felt before on a job.

Only this wasn't a job.

CONNOR

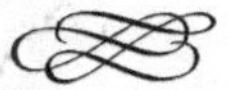

I bristled at James's orders.

No one had the right to speak to me like that. Not anymore.

My feet moved quickly. I was about to tell James that I wouldn't be going anywhere and he wasn't the boss of me when the mess inside the house reminded me exactly why I probably should listen to him.

When I'd gone through the door earlier and seen everything broken after being ripped from the walls and thrown off shelves, each piece of furniture pushed out of place, I hadn't really comprehended what had happened.

In my mind, the state of the house reflected perfectly how I felt inside, and in a perverted way, I'd been relieved to see that, despite all the mess around me, the world hadn't crumbled. I was still here.

Yes, I'd definitely been in shock then because now all I could think was that someone had come into my space, my home, my sanctuary, and ripped it apart.

"Connor?"

I looked at James. His frown created a little crease between his eyes making him look so much more like the serious, grumpy bodyguard and less like my childhood friend. Except I knew how those hazel eyes shone brightly when he was happy and laughing so hard he couldn't help snorting.

"Yes...um...okay. Can I just settle Bubbles in the sink and then we can look around?"

He nodded. I went over to the shattered tank and picked a number of rocks, making sure to use the remaining water in the tank to wash off any bits of glass. Fortunately, they looked clean.

"You should wash your hands. Turtles can carry salmonella," I told James and watched him disappear down the hall toward the bathroom.

I still had a gallon of de-chlorinated water left from the last time I cleaned Bubbles' tank, so I poured it into the kitchen sink, piled the rocks together to make a little platform, and settled Bubbles in.

"No escaping," I said as I saw her going straight for the rocks. I made sure they were as far from the edge as possible before making my own way to the bathroom to wash my hands.

"I'm so sorry, Con."

James's tight voice mirrored exactly how I felt. If the rest of the house was a mess, it didn't compare to what had been done to my bedroom.

All my bedsheets had been ripped off and the mattress underneath was slashed open, the springs poking out everywhere. The curtains had been torn down so hard that one side of the pole had come off from the wall.

I wanted to say something. Swear, shout, anything, but all the air left my lungs.

"Who...who would do this?" I struggled to say.

James put his arm around me and pulled me in for a hug. I took a deep breath in the hope of taking some of his calm and strength.

"We'll figure it out, sweetie, but I need you to look at everything carefully. Are you missing anything?"

I looked around, taking stock of the damage as I went along and then shook my head. "No, everything is here."

"Do you have a duffle bag or a suitcase? Let's put some of your clothes in it before we go through the rest of the house."

I grabbed my old, ratty duffle from the closet and started filling it with the clothes that had remained inside the drawers. Somehow, picking things up off the floor felt as though I was scrambling to get out of my own home rather than choosing to stay away of my own accord.

What a fucked up rationale.

Nothing was missing from the bathroom when I went in to put my toiletries in a washbag.

Everywhere I looked, it was the same, even in the closet in the hallway. Nothing was gone, just carelessly tossed aside.

We went into the guest room that doubled as my office, and that's when I noticed the first thing so far that was out of place, and it stood out because it *wasn't* out of place.

"James," I called to get his attention. "Look."

He came over and stood next to me. "What am I looking at?"

"My desk. Isn't it weird?" I asked, looking at the carefully placed items.

"What? That you grew up to learn pens go inside the case and paper goes in the folder?"

I elbowed him and he chuckled.

"No, Jackass. That's exactly it. I'm as messy as I've ever been."

He looked at me, his worried expression back on.

I went to pick up the tidy pile of bills I'd been working on yesterday when James grabbed my hand.

"Wait, let me take some photos first. We'll need to show Scott these. Maybe it'll give us a clue"

Once James was satisfied that he'd taken enough photos of the paperwork, the desk, and the surrounding areas, I was able to go through it. The only weird thing was the bills were stacked in date order of when they'd arrived in the mail.

The living room and kitchen, which were one open-plan space, were the same mess as the rest of the house.

Suddenly, I couldn't bear to be in the house anymore. Despite my initial reluctance to follow James's instructions, now, all I wanted was to leave, and I didn't even care where I'd end up tonight.

We picked up a new tank, water, and a UV light for Bubbles before James drove us to the Old Mill.

I'd only ever seen the building from a distance whenever I stopped at Benny's Diner for a meal, but I knew the place was special to my brother and his fiancé because it was where they'd met and fell in love a year ago.

"Can't believe it's been a year."

"Since when?" James asked.

"Sorry, I didn't realize I said that out loud," I said, feeling my cheeks heat up.

I looked at James, and he was staring back at me. Twelve months since everything in my life had crumbled to pieces, and I wasn't even sure if the biggest piece had been finding and losing my best friend all over again in a matter of days after all the years apart.

"Shall we go in? Bubbles needs to keep warm."

Yes, I was a coward using the turtle to avoid starting that particular conversation.

I was surprised to see James had a two-bedroom apartment all to himself, but then he explained their set up was to make sure the two love birds had a bodyguard staying on either side of their tiny apartment.

"So, you're saying both you and Ryan have a two-bed apartment while the prince of Lydovia has a small one bedroom?" I asked, settling Bubbles in her tank on the floor and turning the UV light on. She gravitated to the warmth of the light as soon as the glow hit her rock platform. I'd let her warm up first before giving her some food.

"Kris isn't like everyone else you know, and he's certainly nothing like any other royal," James said.

"You know many other royals for comparison?"

My comment was meant as a tease, but I didn't miss James's shoulders tense.

"I'll order some pizza in, if that's okay. It's probably not wise to leave Princess Turtle to her own devices if we go across the road to Benny's," he said, avoiding the question as if it hasn't been asked.

"Sure, I'm happy with that."

"Double cheese and pepperoni?"

I said, "and pineapple" at the same time as James said, "no pineapple."

We looked at each other and smiled, the little tension created by my comment dissipating immediately.

"Looks like we're getting two pizzas," he said.

"You can always pick the pineapple off."

James's eyes went wide. "No pineapple shall touch my cheese, *or* my pepperoni for that matter."

I raised a brow and saw his ears go pink when he realized what he'd just said.

"Do you remember that time we skipped the last period to eat pizza when you found that twenty-dollar bill on the floor?"

"Man, we ate so much pizza I thought I'd have to roll my way home." I laughed.

What I hadn't told James was that I hadn't found the bill on the street. I'd worked washing all my neighbor's cars to earn the money. When James had told me he'd never had pizza from Benny's, I'd made it my mission to make it happen.

My parents had always been amazing, but with three children to raise, sometimes it was hard to give us all an allowance. As the eldest, I wanted to set an example and work for the things I wanted. It hadn't been too hard since most neighbors were happy to pay quite well to keep their front lawns clear of leaves in the autumn and their cars clean.

"I'll go take a shower while we wait for the pizzas if that's okay," I said.

"Connor?" James called before I reached the hallway leading to the bedrooms. "You should call your family."

"I know. I...I'll do it after my shower."

"Okay."

There it was again that look of concern in his eyes. I forced myself to ignore it and went to the guest room.

JAMES

When I heard the shower running, I felt like I could finally breathe for the first time in years.

Going around Connor's house to assess the damage was so painful because I got to see it from his point of view. All of his belongings and his personal space violated by an unknown criminal.

I had to remind myself that both Connor and Bubbles were safe, and I would do anything to help him find who broke into his home and why.

Bubbles was happily dozing under the warm UV light, so I took the opportunity to check in with Kris and Charlie next door.

"Keep an eye on him, Princess. I'll be right back."

When Ryan opened the door to the apartment next to mine, I saw a large pizza and a smaller one in front of Charlie.

"What is it with you Williams men and pineapple on pizza?" I said shuddering at the thought of pineapple on pizza.

Charlie dropped the slice he was about to put in his mouth straight away.

"Oh my god, James, I've been so worried. Where's my brother? Is he okay?"

51

Kris, fortunately, put his arm around Charlie, which helped calming him down, though his worry was still clear by the look on his face and the way he held his shoulders.

"Connor is okay. He's next door, actually."

I put both my hands up and saw Kris tightening his hold on Charlie, hopefully to stop him from running next door to his brother.

"Honestly, Charlie, he is okay. I, on the other hand, may need a new finger after meeting his three-inch terror."

Ryan snorted.

"I mean his turtle," I clarified quickly, but it didn't help because Ryan let out the laugh he'd been trying to contain.

The whole ridiculous conversation seemed to relax Charlie even more. He'd been around me enough in the last three months to know when he needed to hear what I had to say because it could put his safety in jeopardy.

"Connor's house was turned upside down by whoever broke in. That's why he's staying with me." I didn't want to admit that the thought of leaving Connor on his own at his place made my stomach turn.

"Are you sure he's okay?" he asked as if he still wasn't sure.

I hated to see Charlie so worried. He was one of the kindest people I'd ever met, and he always thought of everybody else first. I'd seen that first hand a year ago when he put his life in the press firing line for Kris. I had a lot of respect for him.

"He's a little shaken up, as is to be expected. Why don't we all catch up tomorrow and then you can see Connor for yourself."

Charlie beamed. "Yes! Let's have breakfast at Benny's tomorrow."

"Sounds like a plan, it's been years since I've had Momma Ruth's pancakes," I said.

"Oh yes, I've had those sinful pancakes," Kris said, rubbing his nonexistent belly. "I always need to up my workouts every time I come to Chester Falls."

"I have an idea about how you can work out the extra calories," Charlie said, wiggling his eyebrows.

"And that's my cue. See you in the morning guys," I said.

"I'll follow you, I've had enough pizza anyway," Ryan said.

I suspected he just wanted to leave the love birds alone because he closed the lid on his pizza box before he snatched it up and brought it out with him.

"Hey," he said after closing the apartment door. "Let me know if you need any help, okay? I'll keep an eye on those two in there."

"Thanks, man, really appreciate it," I said before heading back to my apartment.

I'd met Ryan during our Special Forces qualification training. We hadn't served together until a few years later but had remained friends. I trusted him to keep Kris and Charlie safe.

The man had an uncanny way of reading people, something that had served him well in combat until, like me, an injury had put an end to his career.

I locked those thoughts about the end of my own career in the back of my brain before I walked back inside the apartment.

When Connor came into the kitchen after his shower, three things happened: my pulse increased, my dick swelled, and all moisture left my mouth.

He had on a tight Yale University t-shirt that showed how much he still worked out. It was almost threadbare from numerous washings and had a couple of small holes that showed his smooth skin beneath.

His dark copper hair was still wet from his shower and sticking up at odd angles as if he'd run a towel through it to dry it and done nothing else.

I should have taken my eyes from him, but I was a sucker for punishment. Or maybe my new thing was straight guys because I kept looking down at where his sweatpants rode low on his hips.

Fuck. Me. Why did they have to be grey? Did the guy not know anything?

Connor seemed oblivious to my internal struggle because he sat down on the opposite side of the breakfast bar and opened the pizza box marked with a pineapple stamp.

"Hmmm, this smells delicious," he said, taking a slice and looking at me before adding, "Aren't you eating yours? Or did they make a mistake and put pineapple on that one too?"

"Um...no, mine's good."

I opened my box and picked up a slice. The first one tasted of nothing because my brain was too focused on imagining what was under Connor's sweatpants, and if the bulge was anything to go by, I wouldn't be disappointed.

Stop it, James. What the fuck are you doing? You're not going to be disappointed because you're not even going there.

By the third slice, the cheesy flavor of Benny's stone-baked pizza was settling nicely in my stomach, and I'd regained control over my blood flow.

"So, Yale..." I said.

"Yeah, Psychology."

I stopped my slice midway to my mouth. "Wow, Connor, that's amazing. I never knew you were interested in Psychology."

"Well, there's a lot you...nevermind," he said looking away.

I knew what he wasn't saying. There was a lot I didn't know about him.

Maybe it was time to come clean.

"Help me clear this up, and I'll tell you a story," I said.

It didn't take long to put the rest of the pizza in the fridge, though I kept my portion well away from the pineapple abomination it was now sharing a box with, and there was no washing since we'd pretty much eaten out of the box.

Before he joined me on the sofa, Connor took out a small lettuce leaf from the fridge and gave it to Bubbles, who seemed to be loving her new home and hadn't escaped yet.

"Okay," he said, sitting sideways on the sofa so he could face me. "Tell me your story."

"You know how it was always just me and my mom, right?"

He nodded.

"That day. The day we...the day I..." I took a deep breath. "When I got home, my mom was packing our stuff. She just said we were going to live with my dad. We had a car picking us up the next morning."

I ran my hands through my short hair, the memory of the day that changed my life as painful as the day itself.

Connor put his hand over mine and squeezed it gently.

"Don't tell me. Maybe another day, James. It's enough for me to know it wasn't your choice."

His green eyes were so full of sincerity that it made me want to cry. This was the moment I'd waited my whole life for and didn't know it.

I never expected to see my best friend again, but after our first encounter a year ago, I'd lost all hope that he'd ever give me a chance to explain.

"You have to believe me, Con. I didn't want to go. I begged her to stay. I said I could quit school and get a job so I could help out with the bills, but she'd made up her mind."

"Shhhh, that's okay. Tell me the rest another day, okay?" he said.

I nodded and pulled him in for a hug that felt every little bit like I finally had my friend back.

"Did you go to college?" he asked.

"Yeah, Harvard. That's where I met Kris."

Connor chuckled. "How did two kids whose life purpose was to eat all the ice cream in the world end up going to ivy league colleges?"

"I don't know about you, but I lived and breathed school-work while I counted down the days before I could leave for college."

"Me too," he said. "Well, not the counting down the days to leave home part, but the burying my head in books to get my scholarship."

I looked down at where he still had his hand on mine. He squeezed it gently.

"I missed you, James. So much. I used to go to the library after school every day hoping that maybe one day you'd be there, waiting for me..."

Connor took a deep breath and ran his hands over his face, stifling a yawn.

"I really appreciate what you did today. All of it," he said.

"I wouldn't have had it any other way. Now let's turn in because we're having breakfast with the love birds next door tomorrow."

Connor smiled wide as we both said at the same time, "Pancakes!"

CONNOR

"Hey Momma Ruth, look who's here," Benny called out to the kitchen as soon as he saw me, James, Charlie, and Kris walking in Benny's Diner.

He came out from behind the counter to greet us, giving me, Charlie, and Kris a big bear hug.

"Now you, I know your face," Benny said looking at James.

"You must be senile, Benny, if you can't recognize our sweet little Jamie Lexington," Momma Ruth said, approaching us. I noticed James didn't correct her on the surname, but there was still a sliver of tension just like when I'd mentioned it yesterday.

Had James married and taken his husband's name? And why did he look so uptight when his old surname was mentioned?

Momma Ruth's first hug was dished out to James, who despite her calling him little, was anything but since he towered over her by a few feet.

"Hey, Momma Ruth, you're looking good. Whatcha still doing with this old man?" James quipped back at Benny but winked over her head to the man who was like a surrogate uncle to all the kids in Chester Falls.

"Don't you give her any ideas, Jamie," Benny said. "Now, why don't you boys take a seat, and I'll grab you all some coffee."

As soon as we sat down, Charlie's eyes were on me like he was struggling to contain all the questions inside him. When we'd met outside the apartments before coming over to the diner, he'd thrown himself at me as if he hadn't seen me for years instead of just a few months.

Luckily for me, a small touch from Kris was all it took for Charlie to agree to wait until we sat down for breakfast before barraging me with all his questions. Or brunch, because as it turned out, I'd slept like the dead and didn't wake up until after ten.

I couldn't even remember when was the last time I'd overslept like that. My first thought as soon as I saw the time on my phone was to worry about work before I remembered I'd requested the day off because I'd intended on getting drunk yesterday and to spend today in bed licking my wounds.

No, there was no point thinking about work right now. There were more important things to deal with, such as the break-in, apologizing to Tom for missing his store opening, reassuring my brother that I was fine, and more importantly, the return of my best friend.

I really wanted to know more about Jamie Lexington who now went by James Bennett. Where had the light-hearted, funny, and sweet Jamie been in the last fifteen years that made him so gruff, quiet, and like he carried some kind of pain inside?

"So, I think it's safe to say it'll be pancakes all round," I said, not bothering to look at the menu, hoping the talk about food would distract my brother long enough.

I was wrong. Benny hadn't even filled our coffee mugs when my brother leaned over the table a little to catch my eye.

"Okay, I'm not going to pretend to be chill about this anymore, Connor," he said.

"Baby, you haven't been chill since we couldn't find Connor yesterday," Kris said with a laugh, but then stopped when Charlie gave him a murderous look.

"Let's park the break-in issue for a moment. Where were you yesterday, and why did you miss Tom's pre-opening party?"

There was as much worry in his voice as there was anger, and it was very justified.

"I'm so sorry. I will apologize to Tom. I didn't mean to miss his party..." I sighed. "I had a shit day at work and needed to get away. I'm not sure if I thought the party was today or if I was so self-absorbed in my own shitstorm that I forgot."

I ran my hands through my hair, not wanting to look at Charlie because I wasn't sure I could handle him being disappointed with me. I was feeling a lot of that myself already.

"Tom isn't upset with you, Con. But we were really worried when we couldn't get hold of you and then we found out your place had been broken into." Charlie's voice was so full of worry, but I didn't know how to reassure him.

Benny interrupted the conversation when he brought the coffee over and took our order, which not surprisingly, contained a large amount of pancakes and various toppings.

"My phone died. I didn't mean to worry anyone. And I didn't know about the break-in. You have to believe me."

James put his hand on my arm. My breath caught when I looked at him. With the sun behind him, his dark blond hair looked lighter and his hazel eyes much brighter than before. He was looking at me like he knew exactly how I felt and was figuring out a way to let me off.

"We know that, Con," he said and then turned to Charlie. "The priority, now, is to find whoever broke into Connor's place."

"James, what do you need from us?" Kris asked.

"I'd like Connor to stay with me until this is resolved, but that means I can't be with you," James said.

"We have Ryan with us. Do what you need to," Kris reassured me.

"You know it means you need to stick together so he can protect you both," I said, even though I knew Kris took our security precautions seriously.

"I don't think that will be a problem, do you, sweetheart?" Kris said, pulling Charlie closer and kissing his temple.

Charlie still looked like he had questions, but Benny's timely interruption brought the conversation to a temporary ending. Temporary because I knew Charlie wouldn't let go. I'd seen his determination twelve months ago when he seemed to just know I wasn't okay, and I could see it now.

"Man, these are exactly as I remember. No wonder Benny worships the ground Momma Ruth walks on," James said as he tasted his pancakes with scrambled eggs and bacon.

"I would surrender my royal title in a heartbeat if me having these delicious pancakes depended on it," Kris said.

I'd expected Charlie to add his own compliment to Momma Ruth's pancakes, but he looked at me and just smiled. He'd cut his chocolate chip pancake tower down the middle and was nearly finished with one half.

I looked at my blueberry and cream pancakes, and it was only then I realized I'd done exactly the same. God, when was the last time I'd shared pancakes with my brother like we'd done so many times as kids because we'd decided it was better to have just half a pancake but two flavors?

A few more bites were all it took for us to finish one half and then we swapped plates. The still-warm chocolate chips put an instant smile on my face. Charlie's expression mirrored mine as he ran a forkful of pancake over the cream and put it in his mouth, rolling his eyes in delight.

We high-fived each other and laughed, all tension disappearing as I looked at Kris and James who were both smiling at us too.

"I love putting a smile on my handsome boys," Momma Ruth said, approaching our table. "You let me know if you want seconds, all right?"

She put her hand on the one I had resting on the table and squeezed it before she left again toward the kitchen.

"How did you find Connor?" Charlie asked.

I looked at my brother who was leaning into Kris as if he could fall asleep from all the food. His question had been directed at James, who looked at me unsure of what to say.

"I was at the cave," I said.

Charlie stood up straight and crossed his hands on the table leaning slightly forward.

"I've been there before, so I figured it was the one place I could try to find Connor if everything else failed," James said.

Kris looked down at the table with a smile on his face, and Charlie looked utterly puzzled. Time to get him out of his misery.

"James was in my class in high school. We were friends until he moved away...um, we used to hang out at the cave sometimes."

Charlie looked at James and me before going back to James and then Kris, who looked decidedly guilty. Did he know this?

"Baby, it wasn't my story to tell," Kris said and then put his arm around my brother.

Jamie scratched his short scruff and then exhaled. "I told Kris about the best friend I'd lost one night when we got drunk at a party in our dorm at college. It didn't take long for him to figure out who that friend was last year when we met all your family."

The reminder that I'd been in a relationship with the person who'd been responsible for so much hurt in my family was like a bucket of ice water being dumped on me.

"Wait," Charlie said, forcing me to come out of my thoughts and look at him as he pointed a finger at James while he stared at me. "Is James the person you were always getting in trouble for?"

JAMES

I noticed Connor stiffen beside me, but he seemed to come out of it as soon as Charlie chortled.

"I thought you had a secret girlfriend."

"Why would you think that?" Connor asked.

"Well, because you were late to dinner all the time, and you never said where you were and always avoided answering questions. And then there were all the extra jobs you did to earn money. I thought you wanted to take a girl out on dates."

Connor went a little pale at the implication that I was his would-be girlfriend. I couldn't deny his reaction hurt a little, but I tried to remind myself that we'd been just friends, and Connor was straight.

It was reasonable for Charlie to have made those assumptions. Fuck, listening to him talking about his brother's actions then, even I would have believed the same thing.

Except we knew there had been no girlfriend. Just a friend. Just. A. Friend.

Connor's expression didn't give anything away as he took the last sip of his coffee and then stood up.

"Don't we need to stop by the police station to see Scott?" Connor asked. "I'm going back to work tomorrow, so I'm going to need to go home to pick up some stuff. Also need to check on Bubbles."

Charlie got up and hugged Connor, who seemed to hold on to his younger brother like they'd just found each other.

"Call me, okay?" Charlie pleaded.

"I will, and since I'm staying with James, you're on turtlesitting duty until we come back."

Connor looked at me and winked.

I snorted a laugh and followed Connor out of the diner.

"I didn't know you had an evil streak in you, Connor Williams," I teased as I fell into step beside him.

"Looks like we have some catching up to do, James Bennett. By the way, you're driving me to my car."

I chuckled. "Yes, sir."

Charlie's words replayed in my head as I drove us to the Falls parking lot where we'd left Connor's car the day before.

Had Connor really got in trouble for hanging out with me? He'd told me a little bit about his parents, brother, and sister back then, and he'd made them sound like a great family. I'd been almost a little jealous that he'd had more than one person to go back to at the end of the day while at my place, it was just me and my mom.

Also, what had Charlie meant about all the extra jobs?

I tried to put my thoughts away because I didn't want to think about Connor finding a way to get money so we could have fun together, have ice cream every day, and the occasional pizza or burger from Benny's. And I definitely didn't want to think of why he might have done it.

Chester Falls Police Station was in the same building as the town hall, so I was thankful Connor had suggested driving his car back to the Old Mill so we would only need to find one parking spot near the town square.

"Can we stop by Fabulize when we're finished at the station? I'd like to see Tom," Connor asked on our way inside the station.

"Of course," I said, opening the door for him.

We were sitting on the hard plastic chairs inside the station, waiting for Scott to be free to see us. Connor's leg was shaking so much I had to put my hand on his knee.

"Are you okay?" I asked.

"Um, yeah...sorry, I just...nevermind."

I didn't like how Connor looked toward the door like he was planning his escape route.

"Connor, in order for me to protect you, I need to know what's on your mind, what's worrying you. Otherwise, I don't know where the threat is coming from," I said, trying to convey the importance of trusting me to keep him safe.

He let out a strained laugh. "There's no threat, James. It was a random break-in. I just want to get the report done so I can contact the insurance agency and find out how much it's going to cost me to replace all my furniture."

I could have called him out on his lie, but I wasn't sure he was lying or if he genuinely thought the break-in was random. Every instinct in me was telling me it wasn't, but I didn't want to worry him, especially when he already seemed a little on edge.

"Connor, James, thanks for coming over," Scott said as he approached us.

I didn't miss his eyes roaming over Connor, who'd stood up as soon as he'd seen Scott.

"Hi, Scott. Have you got the report ready?" I asked, stretching my hand out and shaking it harder than I needed.

"Um, yes of course, please follow me."

The report didn't offer much information. As Scott had explained the day before, he'd had a call in from a neighbor, then driven past and seen the door open. He'd checked it out and saw the door had been kicked in. The rest of the report stated what I already knew and had seen yesterday.

"Connor, did you find anything that seemed odd or out of place when you looked through the house?" Scott asked.

"Not out of place, but my desk was tidy." Connor shrugged as he relayed this bit of information.

"What do you mean?"

I took out my phone to show Scott the photos I'd taken as Connor continued to explain.

"I'm quite disorganized when it comes to my work. A few days ago, I piled all these bills on my desk to sort out over the weekend. I haven't found anything missing, but whoever did this tidied my desk."

Scott looked confused. "Are you serious?"

"No, we thought it would be funny to tidy Connor's desk, take some photos, and then show them to you," I said, trying my best to keep the frustration out of my voice and failing miserably.

"Look," he said. "What do you want me to say? This is not the most usual of MOs for a burglar."

"You don't need to tell us that. What I need to know is if you're going to take this seriously." This time, there was no hiding it because I'd gotten up, knocking my chair on the floor, and put my hands on Scott's desk. "I'm not sure where you come from or what kind of training you've had, but where I come from, we pay attention to the unremarkable details because those are the ones which will make the difference between someone greeting their family at the airport with a smile or in a box."

Scott's face hardened, but when he spoke his voice was calm and controlled.

"Please sit down, Captain Bennett."

I did and waited for him to go off on one for my behavior considering I was in his office. Instead, he spoke to Connor.

"Connor, my apologies. You have my word that we will do everything we can to find out who did this. If there is anything else at all that you can tell me, or something unusual happens in the next few days, please call me as soon as you can."

Connor nodded. He was holding the report with both hands on his lap and looking down at it. I touched his arm, and he seemed to come out of his head.

"Scott, um...I just want my family to be safe."

Scott looked at me, and I noticed the tiniest change in his expression.

"I will do everything I can. Hannah is helping us today, so if you want to say hi, she's just next door."

Connor smiled wide at the knowledge his sister was in the same building.

"Go on and see Hannah. I'll join you in a minute," I reassured him.

The door had barely closed behind Connor when Scott spoke again. This time, there was none of the gentle officer that had reassured Connor. He was every bit the police officer.

"Captain Bennett, I respect what you did for our country. Hannah is a good friend, so by extension, her family is too. This means I am aware of your position within the Lydovian royal family. If you weren't head of security, I would tell you we are both on the same side here, but if you question my position, credentials, or experience one more time, I will not only rip you a new one, I will also show you exactly where I did my training. As you are, all I can say is thank you for your contribution, Captain Bennett. Are we clear?"

I stood up and held out my hand. "Crystal, Officer LaCruz."

Scott ran his hand over his buzz cut hair and then leaned back on the cabinet behind his desk.

"My gut feeling is that whoever did this knows Connor. The break-in looks like a warning, so I would keep Connor very close."

"Agreed," I said before making my way to the office next door. As much as I disliked how Scott has spoken to me, I was also relieved he was strong enough to stand up to a man almost twice his size and double his weight. Also smart enough to do it from behind his desk. I could come to like officer LaCruz.

Hannah's office door wasn't closed, so I could hear their conversation.

"I'm glad you're okay, Con. Don't worry, Scott is great, and he'll find out who did this in no time," Hannah said.

"Yeah, he seems really good."

"Now, what I want to know is, what's up with Superman out there."

I was about to enter the room before Hannah's almost whisper stopped me. I didn't know why, but I wanted to hear what Connor's response was.

"What do you mean?" he asked.

"James, you dumbass. The man ran like a bat out of hell yesterday to look for you."

CONNOR

"What do you mean?" I asked my sister who had that glint in her eye that always scared me a little.

"Has something happened between you?" she asked.

"What? No. What kind of question is that?"

"Stop answering a question with a question," she said, sitting forward and crossing her arms over her desk. "You two looked like you were ready to kill each other a year ago, and now he's—"

Thankfully a knock on the door followed by James stepping into the room stopped Hannah from continuing her questioning.

"Hey, Hannah," James said before turning to me. "Do you want to stop by Spilled Beans and grab Tom a coffee?"

"Yes! Definitely," I said, nearly jumping off my chair.

"Do you mind if I join you? I promised Ellie I'd have lunch with her in the square," she said.

"Of course," I said.

Spilled Beans was busy as usual at lunchtime, and Indy, my friend and owner of the small coffee shop, was busy making drinks behind the counter while his assistant, Jake, served their amazing pastries.

"God, I need this line to move so I can get my eyes on today's special cupcake," Hannah said as she got on the tips of her toes to see over people's shoulders.

I moved over to the side to see if I could put my sister out of her misery but forgot James was right next to me.

"Crap, sorry," I said quickly. "Didn't mean to—"

"That's okay," James said, his voice smooth and deep like full-bodied whiskey. He smelled really good. How did he manage to smell like he'd just got out of the shower all the time?

"Connor."

I jumped away from James when I heard someone calling my name.

All blood drained from my face, and my words became stuck in my throat.

"Linda, hi. How have you been?"

"Unemployed," she said with a totally justified accusation in her voice.

"I'm sor—"

"Your words don't mean a thing anymore, so save them for someone who cares."

Her parting comment felt so heavy on me I wasn't sure I could hold myself upright anymore.

"Do you mind if we go?" I asked James.

"Sure."

I kissed my sister on the cheek and promised I'd see her soon.

James was right behind me, as I knew he would be, but instead of getting in the driver seat of his car, he followed me to the passenger side.

I opened the door as soon as he unlocked it and got in. James crouched down between me and the opened door.

His touch was as gentle as his voice when he spoke. "Hey, are you okay? What happened over there?"

"I fired her. That woman in the coffee shop. Her husband is on disability and she has two teenage sons, and I fired her."

I couldn't have stopped the tears if I'd wanted to. My breakfast threatened to come out, so I leaned over with my elbows on my knees and rested my head on my hands, trying to take deep breaths.

"It's okay." James's soothing voice helped to calm me down a little, but it was his touch that made me look up to him as he ran his fingers through my hair.

"It's not okay. How can I live with myself knowing someone is struggling to put food on the table because of me."

"Connor, listen to me. First of all, even though I don't know what happened, I have no doubt that you tried to do everything you could to keep that woman in her job. And second, she was in a coffee shop... buying coffee. She's okay, Connor."

I wanted to argue, but James held both my hands in his and squeezed them. It felt so good to have someone in my corner that I relished in it for an extra few seconds.

"Do you really need to go to your place? I can take you furniture shopping, or we can just go back to the apartment and see what Princess Turtle is up to."

"That would be really nice," I said, wiping my damp face with my shirt sleeve.

"Which one?"

"Take a guess," I joked.

"Princess Turtle it is," he said with a wink. My heart skipped a beat at both his playfulness and mind reading skills. God, it was good having my friend back.

We heard the argument before we even turned the corner of the corridor into the open plan living room and kitchen of James's apartment.

I raised my hands to James and then gestured for him to not make a noise.

"She needs to learn!" I heard Charlie say.

"Baby, she's a turtle."

Kris's voice was as calm as ever, and I suspected he was running his hand over Charlie's back, which was something I'd seen him do many times.

"So, you're on her side now," Charlie said.

"Um no, that's not—" Kris tried to say, but Charlie interrupted.

"Is this how it's going to be when we have children?" Charlie said. Exasperation clear in his voice.

I looked at James, and he was struggling to contain his laughter too. I could just imagine poor Kris's face as Charlie admonished him for taking sides with a tiny turtle.

"Bubbles, listen to Uncle Charlie," he said, sounding frustrated. I dared to peek around the corner, hoping they were facing the other way. "We don't run away, and we don't bite people. Repeat after me."

Charlie was pointing a stern finger at Bubbles, who was staring back as though she really was paying attention. Kris was shaking his head.

"We. Don't. Run. And. We. Don't. Bite."

James snorted behind me, giving our presence away. I elbowed him a little too hard, making him cough out his laugh.

I went over and kneeled down on the floor, picking Bubbles up and placing her on my palm.

"Have you been a naughty girl for Uncle Charlie and Uncle Kris?" I cooed at her while I scratched her head and then her carapace just where she liked.

James gave me a new lettuce leaf from the fridge, so I placed Bubbles in the separated part of the tank designated for when she was eating. It wasn't until Bubbles took her first bite that I realized I hadn't asked for the lettuce. I looked at James and he smiled but then looked away and sat on the sofa.

"How were things at the station?" Charlie asked sitting back into Kris's embrace.

I sighed, not wanting to say what I'd been refusing to accept.

"I think whoever did it is someone that knows me well."

Charlie gasped. "Are you sure?"

"No, but there's nothing missing, so it can't be a random break-in and then..."

"Then what?" Charlie asked.

I looked at James. He had that focused look in his eyes again like he was on the job.

"I bumped into someone today. Someone who worked for my company and who lost their job because of me."

"Do you think they did it, Connor?" Kris asked.

"No, not her. Linda was angry with me, and she was right to be, but I don't think she'd do anything."

"Are you thinking someone else would be angry enough to come after you?" James asked.

I shrugged my shoulders.

"Do you know the names of everyone you had to fire?" James asked.

"Yes." They were imprinted in my head and there was no way I'd ever forget the day I had to tell all the people I'd built relationships with that they wouldn't have a job anymore.

James followed my brother and Kris out so he could catch up with Ryan. Once Bubbles had had her food and I'd cleaned the part of the tank where she ate, I found myself with nothing to do.

If I was home, I could start clearing up the mess, or at the very least, look for more clues. Was it possible that someone I'd worked with was doing this to me?

The more I thought about it, the more afraid I became that whoever ransacked my apartment would also target my family. Fear led to frustration at the unknown danger, and after that, I was just angry.

"Con?"

James was by the door of my bedroom looking worried.

"What?" I said, letting my frustration out on him.

"I should be asking that," he said, his eyes narrowing, and thankfully ignoring how I'd reacted. "You were pacing the room back and forth. Has anything happened?"

I shook my head. "I need to go back to my place."

"No. It's not safe."

"I'm not going to be driven out of my own home by anyone,

and definitely not by someone who doesn't have the guts to threaten me to my face."

James crossed his arms and that just annoyed me even more, so I walked over until I was nose to nose with him.

"I am not scared of them, of anyone. Do you hear me?" I knew I was shouting now, and James's lack of reaction was fuel to my displaced anger.

"I don't need a bodyguard, and I can drive myself. You can come with me, or you can stay. I don't care," I shouted as I picked up my keys from the dresser.

I'd been happy to be the vehicle for Connor to vent out his anger and frustration. The louder he shouted at the invisible threat, the more I saw of my old friend. This was the Connor I'd known and missed.

The Connor that didn't take any crap from anyone and who stood up for himself on and off the pitch.

Whatever happened with him had knocked his confidence. Maybe it was the shitstorm with his ex-girlfriend, or maybe his job was a bigger problem than he had let on, but I was glad to finally see some fight in him.

"And I'm going to go back to work tomorrow," he said as his final and non-negotiable parting words.

I bit the inside of my cheek to stop from smiling, even though it was another part of my anatomy that had woken up with Connor's rant.

"Sorry to break it to you, but you're not going to work tomorrow," I said.

His green eyes were as stormy as I'd ever seen them, so before he had a chance to come at me, I clarified, "Tomorrow is Saturday."

He let out a long breath and sat on his bed. I sat next to him and said, "I don't know grown-up Connor all that well, but teenager Connor wouldn't be seen dead at school on a Saturday. Well, not unless there was football practice, that is."

"You're right," he said. "Teenage James was more likely to forget it was Saturday and turn up at school anyway."

I poked him in the ribs. "That was only once, and fuck you. I loved school."

He used my move to grab my arm and put me in a headlock.

"You just wanted to hang out with me because I was so cool," he said.

I tried to get out of the headlock, but Connor was stronger than I'd expected, so I had to employ a different tactic. While he was distracted trying to ruffle my short hair, I grabbed him by the waist and pinned him down with my legs.

"I think you were the one who wanted to hang out with me. Let's face it, your IQ went up by a few points just by sitting next to me." I knew he knew I didn't mean anything by it. All the time we'd spent studying together, he'd always proven that while he would have preferred to be playing football, he was actually really smart.

"I had a reputation to uphold," he said.

"Oh yeah, Hotshot? And what was that?" I said at the same time as Connor raised his hips, a move that distracted me long enough that he was able to overturn us so I was the one who ended up with my back on the bed.

I closed my eyes, wishing desperately that he wouldn't move, because if he did, there was no way he wouldn't feel how hard I was.

When Connor's phone rang and he got off me to pick it up, I turned on my belly and said a little prayer of thanks to whomever had interrupted us.

"Oh, hey man," Connor said to the person on the other side of the line.

I got up to go to the bathroom attached to my bedroom, only paying a little bit of attention to the phone call. It sounded like he was talking about football, so it was nothing for me to worry about.

What had me more worried was that I was still painfully hard, and there was no doubt what I'd be doing as soon as I closed the door behind me.

It was unprofessional and all kinds of wrong, but my body hadn't gotten the memo that it wasn't okay to be attracted to a straight man, or an old friend for that matter.

I didn't bother undressing because I knew it wouldn't take long to bring myself to climax with only a few strokes of my cock. When was the last time I'd been so hard for someone?

The answer was never. I looked down at the small wet patch on my boxer shorts and nearly came at the sight of it. My cock was so hard it was raising the elastic waistband of my underwear. I pressed my hand over it and squeezed, imagining Connor's tentative touch doing the same.

In my head, I wasn't touching myself. Connor was there, on his knees, one hand running up and down my back before settling on the globes of my ass while the other teased my erection.

"Fuck, yes..." I hissed.

As I finally wrapped my fist around my length and then teased the head with my thumb, spreading my pre-come in that sensitive area, it wasn't my hand anymore, it was Connor's. And then it wasn't his hand, it was his mouth. As soon as I imagined the heat from his mouth and the look of pure lust in his green eyes as he took me in, I couldn't hold it in any longer. I came so hard that some of it hit the bathroom mirror above the sink.

My slacks were pooled by my feet so I stepped out of them, but my boxer shorts didn't even make it past my ass.

For someone who kept a strict fitness regime, I was struggling to get my breathing back to normal. I cleaned my hands and wiped the mirror before I sat down on the floor with my back to the sink cabinet.

I was in serious trouble, and not just because being attracted to someone I was trying to protect was wrong on every level, but because this was Connor, and Connor would always be more than just a friend to me. That meant my heart was at stake, and I needed to tread these waters very carefully because I couldn't go through the pain of losing Connor again.

Maybe I should get back to work and focus on finding any clues to the identity of the person, or persons, that broke into Connor's house. That way, I could go back to my real job.

With my eyes fixed on the floor in front of me, I didn't see my attacker until she'd stuck her beak into the fleshy part of my hand between my little finger and my wrist.

"Fuck, shit," I cried as I tried to hold her with my other hand so she'd release me.

The bathroom door slammed open, and it was like one of those moments that happen in slow motion in movies. Bubbles was latched onto my hand, Connor's eyes fixed onto Bubbles, and I looked from her to him wondering when she'd let go and waiting for the moment he'd realize I was sitting on my bathroom floor with my underwear halfway down my ass.

Fuck, I was never going to live this down.

"Bubbles, what the hell!" Connor said, kneeling next to me. "I'm so sorry, James. I didn't think she'd escape again."

"That's okay. Just help me get my hand back."

"Come on now, Bubbles," Connor said gently. "Let's leave Uncle James alone again so he can carry on doing what he was doing before you barged in."

"I wasn't...I..." My face felt hot as I tried hopelessly to cover my crotch with my shirt.

I didn't think it was possible to get any more embarrassed, but when my dick perked up again because Connor had his hands on mine soothing the skin that Bubbles had nearly punctured, I nearly died on the spot. Especially because Connor picked that moment to look down at where there was still some left over cum from my solo session now mixed with a new wet spot.

"I'm so sorry. I...um, I'll leave you...we'll just...um...go," he said avoiding eye contact, for which I was grateful.

I closed the door behind Connor and jumped in the shower, hoping to wash off my stupidity and my embarrassment alongside the remains of what I'd done.

When I came out, I hoped to apologize to Connor, but I couldn't see him anywhere. A note on the kitchen table put my mind at ease. He was next door with Charlie.

There was only one thing I could do while I waited for Connor to come back, and that was to have words with Princess Bubbles because I sure as shit couldn't face Connor *and* Charlie right now.

"Okay, Miss Bubbles, me and you need to talk."

My statement was largely ignored by the tiny troublemaker who was swimming in the deeper part of the tank.

"How do you even get out of here?" I looked for any part of the tank that had lower walls she could climb over, but even her rocky beach under the UV light was in the middle of the tank to mitigate potential escape attempts. "You know that tracking device I put in Kris and Charlie's watches? I'm going to put a tiny one on you too."

Since I was still being ignored, I carried on talking. After being caught with my trousers down at my ankles, would it be any worse talking to a turtle? I didn't think so.

"Now, I know you're still a baby girl, so you need to trust me on this rule, okay? It'll serve you well for the future. Stay away from human bathrooms unless you want to be witness to things that your innocent turtle eyes shouldn't see. And bedrooms for that matter...and kitchens. Come to think of it, just stick to your tank from now on, and it'll be better for all of us, okay?" I said.

"How about hallways?" Connor said, leaning against the doorframe.

Fuck. Me.

CONNOR

Watching James talk to my turtle as if she were his little kid did something to me. My chest felt warm like I was coming home, to my real home, the place I belonged and where I would feel safe and protected. Where I could be myself any time, all the time.

I didn't understand what was happening. Well, I did. I wasn't stupid and knew what attraction felt like when it happened. What I didn't get was why it was happening with James.

Was I attracted to him? I wasn't gay. At least I didn't think I was. I'd had plenty of gay friends at college and not for a second had I been attracted to them.

Earlier, when James and I had been messing around on my bed, I'd got painfully hard and would have probably embarrassed myself if my phone hadn't saved me.

After my call, I'd gone to check on Bubbles to see if her tank needed cleaning when I'd found her missing. Again. The worry that she'd get hurt outside the tank had been enough to rush all my blood to my stomach and make me nauseous.

I hadn't even thought twice about barging into James's bathroom when I'd heard him shout. Something I was both glad for, because I'd found my terror of a turtle, and regretted, because it was clear what James had been doing in the bathroom before he was interrupted.

His hand had felt warm and strong under my touch as I soothed the reddened area where Bubbles had bitten.

I hadn't even noticed his state of undress until I felt his hand close over mine, and then it was *all* I saw. His naked thighs, the bulge under his boxer shorts, and the evidence that he'd, in fact, just made himself come with his own hand, the hand I was now holding.

To say I'd flat-out ran out of the bathroom was an understatement because I'd placed Bubbles back in her tank and left the apartment. It was only the thought that James might get worried that made me return to leave him a message.

The sound of the shower coming from the direction of his room had given me a little time to find some paper and a pen.

My intention had been to hide in my brother's apartment for a while and wait for the mortification to go away, but my feet had carried me in the opposite direction.

I'd spent a whole hour walking around the grassy area in front of the Old Mill building, thinking about everything that had happened in the last forty-eight hours.

Benny's Diner across the road was filling up with people going about their daily lives, putting all the worries aside while they enjoyed Momma Ruth's cooking.

When the chill of the early evening permeated through my clothes, I went back to the apartment to face James, but before I could think of anything to say to him, I heard his soft but firm voice.

Unlike earlier, Bubbles was swimming happily in the deeper part of the tank. James sat cross-legged on the floor, his broad shoulders straining the fabric of his shirt.

The James I'd known as a teenager was skinny and didn't know how to fit in his body. This James was confident, a lot less awkward, and very much not skinny anymore.

For all my uncertainty about how to approach the moment in the bathroom earlier, I hadn't accounted for my mouth to speak without permission from my brain.

"What?" James said, his eyes wide open as he turned around and got on his feet as though he had springs inside his legs.

Fuck, Connor backtrack. Back. Track.

"Um...Kris is always saying hallway adult time is the best, so I thought you might want to add it to your list."

Shut up, Connor. Just shut the fuck up.

"No, I don't want to know what they do when...take it back please," James said, closing his eyes and covering his ears, pretending to shiver at the thought.

I chuckled.

"Hey, I forgot I have football practice tomorrow. Do you want to come watch?" I asked.

"Of course. It's been years since I've seen you play."

I laughed but didn't correct him. He'd find out soon enough.

Kris, Charlie, and Ryan came over with Chinese food and the excuse that Charlie wanted to have another chat with Bubbles, but I could see right through my brother.

"So, little brother, tell me about this new house you guys bought and how you're going to convince Kris to build a pond for turtles in the backyard."

Charlie had the decency to blush, but then he took out a little sketch pad from his pocket and sat on the floor drawing Bubbles.

"I see the two amigos are back together," Wren said as I approached him before he told the kids to do a few warm-up laps around the field.

Helping Wren coaching youth football was the highlight of my week, and I waved at all the kids that called out to me as they set off on their warm-up.

"What do you mean?"

"Dude, that guy was your shadow then, and it looks like he's your shadow now. And what a fucking sexy shadow he grew up to be." He winked.

"I wonder what Tom, *your boyfriend*," I said, highlighting each syllable, "would say about that."

"You mean the boyfriend who's shamelessly flirting with your guy over there?"

I turned my head so fast toward the bleachers I nearly pulled a muscle. Wren laughed so loud both James and Tom looked at us. They both waved, and I saw Tom doing a mock sign of the cross and mouthing *thank you* to me. Poor James looked like he wanted to be anywhere else but under the attention of my amazing but-sometimes-too-sparkly friend.

"So, what's the deal with you two?" Wren asked.

"No deal," I said.

"Are you sure? You guys were really close before, I thought..."

I looked back at Wren who looked almost embarrassed. "I thought...I thought something had happened between you two, or in the very least, you'd experimented together."

"Did you know James was gay back then?" I asked.

"I had an idea, but then again, I was struggling with my own bisexuality. It was hard to pay attention to other boys without getting confused."

Wren hadn't come out as bi until he'd met Tom a few months ago. He'd said that he'd stayed in the closet for his career, but after coming back to Chester Falls and falling in love, he didn't feel the need to hide anymore.

"When did you know?" I asked, running my hand down the back of my neck.

"That I was bi?"

"Yeah..."

"Took me a while to really understand it. It wasn't until I was in college that I had the chance to hook up with a guy, so I guess up until then, I thought I was just one of those people who can find beauty in people regardless of gender." He laughed. "I mean,

I still am like that, but now I know what I want to do to them when we're naked."

"And holy mother of pearls, does he know what to do when he's naked."

I didn't need to move my eyes from the kids to know who'd made the comment.

"TMI, Tom," I said.

"Soooo, what's up with the grumpy bodyguard over there?" Tom asked.

"He's not grumpy," I said, feeling that I needed to defend James.

"Then why is he staring at you like he wants to eat you and refusing my awesome brownies?"

This time I did look at Tom, who was pouting as though James refusing to have one of his baked goods was the worst thing he could ever do.

"Maybe if you stop staring at him like you want to cover him with buttercream and lick him all over, he might not look so scared of you," I quipped.

He waved his hand off and wrapped his arms around Wren. "There's only one man I'll ever want to cover in buttercream, but we're not here to talk about what we did last night."

"Tom." I shook my head and looked at Wren who shrugged.

"I'm not even sorry, man. This guy has the best mouth—"

I raised my hand to stop him, but Tom grabbed it and leaned toward me, whispering, "Don't diss it till you kiss it." He then kissed Wren like it was going out of fashion and went back to the table where he'd laid out his homemade brownies and juice for the kids to have after their practice.

"Thank fuck the kids are on the other side of the field," Wren said, doing his best to adjust himself discretely.

Tom's words stayed with me throughout the practice game. Should I kiss James to really find out if my attraction was genuine?

Excitement pooled in my stomach, but then I thought about the last time it had happened and what I'd lost afterward.

JAMES

"I'm going to make you pay for that," I said as I paid attention to the knife in my hand so I didn't end up losing a finger.

"Don't know what you mean," he teased as he got the steak out of the fridge.

"When you mentioned football practice, you forgot that tiny detail about the age group," I said.

"I'll have you know those kids have more talent than many players I've worked with."

"They also have no filter," I said, remembering some of the ridiculous questions I was asked after practice.

How many vegetables do I have to eat to get big muscles like yours? Did your mommy stretch you so you'd be that tall? And my favorite from a little boy that had been told off by Wren for using colorful language, *Why were swear words invented if we're not allowed to say them?*

We'd had a great day, and for the first time since I'd found Connor half-drunk at the cave days ago, he looked happy and relaxed. I suspected coaching the kids had something to do with it since it looked so full-on he probably hadn't had a chance to think of anything else all afternoon.

Just as football practice was winding down, we'd both had a text from Charlie inviting us to dinner at their parents' place, but Connor had said he was beat from practice and wanted a quiet evening in.

We'd settled for making our own dinner instead of ordering in or going to the diner again, so here I was, doing my best to follow Connor's instructions on the perfect technique to cut vegetables for his stir-fry.

"How did you get to coach kids' football?" I asked.

"When I moved back to Chester Falls a year ago, Coach Johnson asked me if I wanted to help him with the kids. I hadn't played in a while, so it was a good incentive to start training again and get involved in something good."

"I remember him," I said. Not that I'd played football in high school, far from it. Sometimes I used to watch Connor play before he walked me to the bus stop.

"He retired a few months ago, so Wren took his place."

"And he's with Tom, right?" I tried to sound nonchalant about it, but in reality, I was curious about Connor's friendship with Wren. Okay, and a little jealous too. I had no right, but I couldn't help how I felt.

"Uh-huh, I've never seen a couple more in love than those two. Well, maybe Charlie and Kris," he said, placing the knife he was cutting the steak strips with on the chopping board. "And Hannah and Ellie, my parents, Uncle John and Aunt Gina..."

His voice kept going lower and lower with each name he called out.

"It was just me that couldn't do it," he whispered.

"Do what?"

"The relationship," he said in such a low voice I was sure it was meant only for himself.

"Hey." I stopped what I was doing, put down my own knife, and turned him to face me. There was a sadness in his eyes, and I didn't know what to do or say to make it go away.

I wanted that vivid forest green staring back at me, not the dark, sad one that had taken hold now. I put my hands on either side of his face, and the tiniest smile graced his lips as I traced the tiny freckles under his eyes.

"With the Sun in Uranus, you have this overwhelming need to feed people. This is a good thing because people are hungry," I said in the same straight voice I used when we were kids and pretended his freckles were stars.

I released him just as he punched me in the stomach.

My heart soared as I saw his cheeky smile back.

"Oh no," I said in mock panic. "You're going to give me food poisoning, aren't you? Maybe I should finish dinner. You go play with Princess Bubbles before she has any ideas of highjacking dinner time with another great escape."

I went back to my dinner preparation duties, but my mind couldn't stop trying to put all the pieces of the Connor puzzle together.

When we were young, he was confident, strong, and self-assured. He handled his schoolwork like he handled his football practice, with hard work and dedication.

I'd expected that Connor would grow up to conquer the world, excel at everything, but also be the guy that was always there for you.

Not to say that he wasn't, and that was what I couldn't understand.

Connor cared about people. The evidence of that was the way he'd been affected by the encounter with his former work colleague. I'd also witnessed first-hand how he was with the kids at practice. He cared about them, and he knew his stuff. I'd bet my life on how great he was at his job too.

"Smells nice," he said, leaning over me to check on dinner. "God, I'm starving."

It was an innocent thing to do, but he was so close that I could smell his shampoo. All I wanted to do was turn the burner off and run my fingers through his hair before I tilted his head up for a kiss.

"It's nearly done. Just need to add the noodles," I said, reaching out for the other pan.

When Connor didn't move more than a few inches, I had no choice but to get in his space to reach for the noodles.

My heartbeat went from stroll-in-the-park to supersonic speed when he looked up at me.

I tried to keep my breathing steady as I put the pan back on the stove and looked at him.

His eyes were wide open and staring right into mine. I wanted desperately to see something in those bright green eyes that matched how I was feeling, but at the same time, I was too scared.

What would happen if I did see something, and what would happen if I didn't?

Connor was so close he became my whole world. I heard his breath catch, smelled his aftershave, saw the confusion and need in his gaze while my fingers fought with me in a battle of wills to touch his skin, and all I wanted more than my next breath was to taste him.

My heart beat so fast I was sure I'd have a stroke if nothing happened in the next few seconds. Connor needed to kiss me or move away because there was no way I'd resist the way he was looking at me, as though he'd made up his mind.

His lips parted and slowly closed again.

For the love of god, Connor, please kiss me.

Connor raised his right hand and placed it on my chest just above my heart. His gaze shot to his hand, no doubt because he could feel the heartbeat beneath.

"I never had a chance to ask you," he said. His voice cracked a little, and his eyes were still on my chest.

"Ask me what?"

"What it meant, how it felt..."

I didn't know what he was talking about, but before I could ask, he spoke again.

"I'm sorry, Jamie."

Him using my childhood nickname caught me off guard. What did he mean?

"What are you sorry for, Connor?"

"Running." His eyes moved from his hand to my lips. "I was scared and confused...I still am."

I placed my hands on either side of his face, but unlike earlier when he'd been upset, now there was something else in his eyes.

"I don't want to run anymore, Jamie."

"Con—" My plea was interrupted by the slamming of his lips on mine.

For the longest time, he didn't move. It couldn't be called a kiss, more that our lips were simply pressed together. When I tried to break it, I opened my mouth slightly, and that was when my whole world changed because Connor took my bottom lip between his and sucked it into his mouth.

All the little hairs on my body stood at attention, my stomach filled with butterflies, and the blood rushed through my veins like it was on fire. Putting it simply, I felt his kiss everywhere.

The soft, slow kisses gave way to what could only be described as two people desperate to taste every bit of each other as if tomorrow was going to be here too quickly, and with the new day, all the magic of this moment would vanish.

I forgot about the turtle. I forgot about dinner. Fuck dinner, I never needed to eat again if I could taste Connor until the end of my days.

His hands fisted my shirt like he didn't trust me to not let go. Not a fucking chance.

I put one arm around his waist while my free hand cradled his neck to keep him in place. I kissed his lips, all the way down his jaw, hearing him gasping for air when I reached the soft skin of his neck and sucked on it.

"This is how it should have been," I whispered in his ear.

We were both breathing heavily, resting our heads on each other's shoulder. Was this really happening? Had Connor Williams just kissed me and let me kiss him back?

CONNOR

What had I just done?

I'd kissed Jamie Lexington. No, I hadn't just kissed him. I'd ravished him.

Even as I tried to catch my breath, my brain was scrambling to understand so many things at the same time that I was surprised I hadn't passed out yet.

How was it possible to have gone my whole life without a kiss like this? And how would I carry on living if it didn't happen again? Did it mean I was gay? Bi? And what the fuck would I do now?

The arm James had around my waist was solely responsible for my current upright position, I was pretty sure of that, while the hand he'd had around my neck slid up and down my back in a gentle motion.

"Connor."

James's voice was soft, speaking directly to a part of me I hadn't known existed. Or maybe it had been dormant, waiting for him.

I shook my head. My hands still gripped his shirt, and my lips still tingled from his touch. I could still taste him in my tongue.

Just a little longer. Give me just this before I have to let you go.

He ran both his hands down my back and then rested them on my hips, forcing me to look at him.

The uncertainty in his eyes mirrored what I felt.

I opened my mouth to say something, but I wasn't sure I could come up with words that were good enough to express how I felt; my confusion, my elation, my relief, my absolute fear.

James released his hold on me and took a small step back. As he did, he nearly knocked the dinner off the stove. I managed to grab the handle just in time.

"Fuck, sorry," he said, running his hand thought his short hair. "We should eat."

"Yeah, sure."

He mixed the noodles with the vegetables and added the steak strips with such dexterity I wondered if he cooked for himself from scratch often.

The next thirty minutes were filled with awkward silence as we ate our meal and then cleared up our plates.

"I'm going to head to my room," he said. "I've got a headache, probably didn't drink enough water today...or something."

"Okay. There's some Tylenol in my bag in the bathroom if you want."

"Yeah, thanks."

I stood in the kitchen feeling empty and alone. Bubbles was asleep under the UV light, so I couldn't use her for something to do.

You know what you need to do Connor.

I stopped in front of the door to James's room and raised my hand to knock.

"James?" I called.

Seconds later, the door opened. He'd changed from his usual white shirt and black slacks and was now wearing grey sweatpants and a well-worn Harvard t-shirt that stretched across his chest and hugged his biceps.

James was beautiful. I think on some level I'd felt the same way when I was only a teenager, but it never occurred to me that what I may have felt was attraction. Quite stupid when both your brother and sister are gay. I couldn't help letting out a choked laugh.

"Do you need anything?" he asked.

"Yes," I said, looking into his eyes.

"What is it?" There was no impatience in his voice.

"I need you to know I don't regret it, but..." I stopped to try and find the right words. "I've never felt anything for another man, James. Ever. And now I have these feelings I don't understand..."

He let out a long exhale and then pulled me into his strong arms. It felt so good I wanted to cry.

"You don't have to figure everything out at once, Con," he said without letting go. "But I have to look after my own heart."

I put some space between us and nodded. "I understand."

Somehow this exchange, even though it hadn't solved anything, made me feel better. James deserved more than someone who didn't have a clue about how to navigate this situation. Hell, even if I knew what I wanted, he still deserved better than me.

As I turned to leave for my room, James called me.

"I need to give Ryan a day off tomorrow. Kris and Charlie are spending the day with your parents."

"Okay, it's been a while since I've had one of my dad's Sunday barbecues."

James laughed. "I've heard the stories."

"They're all true, I'm afraid," I said with an apologetic shrug I didn't mean. It was common knowledge my dad was a terrible cook, but with the right supervision, usually from Uncle John, we'd avoided any major food poisoning incidents so far. "Don't worry, my mom's apple and cinnamon cobbler totally makes up for it."

I took the memory of his smile with me to my bedroom and kept it in my thoughts until I fell asleep.

~

The number of cars parked in my parents' driveway told me this wasn't just any Sunday barbecue.

I sighed, steadying myself for the oncoming questions about the break-in I knew would start the moment I walked through the door.

"What's up?" James asked.

"Nothing, why?"

"I don't know your family that well, apart from Charlie of course, but they seem great. Why are you so tense?"

"Ugh, my family can be a bit much sometimes," I confessed.

James didn't say anything, so I looked at him. His eyes were focused on the mirrors as he maneuvered to park the car, but his face told me he had something to say.

"What?"

He didn't speak until he'd turned the car off, and then he faced me, reaching over the console to touch my arm before he thought better of it and placed his hands on the steering wheel.

"It's a good thing, Connor. Trust me," he said, sounding wistful.

"What do you mean?"

"Never mind, let's go in."

I didn't like how he was suddenly all tense. "No, tell me."

"It's just that...appreciate the family you have, Connor. If they ask questions, it's because they worry, and that means they care," he said getting out of the car.

Did he mean he didn't have a family that cared about him? I'd always known his family was only him and his mom, but I thought they were close.

I caught up with James as he was almost on the steps leading to the front porch. He locked the car from a distance and went to press the doorbell, but the door opened before he could, causing us both to jump.

"Oh, my baby boy," my mom exclaimed before putting her

arms around me. I hugged her back, taking in the scent of her perfume mixed with apple and cinnamon.

"Mom, you smell edible." I chuckled.

"If you think telling me nice things means I'm not going to give you an earful for scaring us like that...you're absolutely right."

I heard James laugh behind me.

"James, sweetheart, it's lovely to see you again, and thank you so much for looking after both of my boys," she said before she gave James the same kind of mom hug.

"It's my job, Mrs. Williams."

"Don't you 'Mrs. Williams' me, young man. It's Caroline, and you take a compliment when you're given one."

"Yes, ma'am," James said.

We exchanged a look and walked through the door together, both with a smile on our faces as we joined the rest of my family in the garden.

The questions didn't last as long as I expected, mainly because James had taken over and explained the situation.

Warmth filled my face when I remembered what I'd done to him last night, and seeing him protecting me against the good intentions of my family after knowing how nervous I'd been earlier just made me want to do it all over again.

"You sneaky devil," Tom whispered after sidling up to me holding a very colorful cocktail. He took a sip, rolling his eyes no doubt from the pleasure of the sugar rush. "You totally kissed him."

"What? No I didn't," I said between my teeth so no one over-heard us.

"That blush on your face and the way you look at him tells me otherwise," he sang as he took another sip of his drink. "You can carry on denying it, but as sure as unicorns are real, you kissed that man."

"Unicorns aren't real," I said in a flat voice.

Tom gasped.

"What's up, babe?" Wren came from behind Tom and wrapped his arms around Tom's waist.

"Connor said unicorns aren't real," he whined with an exaggerated pout.

Wren looked at me, faking shock. "Let's go, babe. You don't need this kind of negativity in your life."

Tom stuck his now blue tongue out at me, and they both went out toward the barbecue area to join my uncle. Wren looked back and winked as I shook my head.

"You look happy," Charlie said, holding up a beer to his lips.

"I'm okay." Movement from the kitchen door grabbed my attention from Charlie.

The last person I expected to see coming through the door and walking at a speed toward me was my best friend Rory.

"Fuck, man," I said bringing him in for a hug. "I missed you. I hope this means you're back for good."

"Sure does," he said with a big grin.

"Hi Rory," James said suddenly, appearing where Charlie had been just moments ago.

JAMES

I'd tried my best to give Connor some space today. He was around his family and seemed a lot more relaxed after I managed to deflect the questions about the break-in.

After that, everyone wanted to know about Bubbles, which gave Charlie a reason to gush over his pet niece and show all the photos he took of her on his phone.

As for me, every single second of last night's kiss had been on replay in my head ever since, so I hadn't had a lot of sleep. That would explain my stupid reaction as soon as I saw Connor's best friend, Rory, cross the garden in his direction.

Rory had been the reason Kris and Charlie had become closer a year ago when Kris offered to stand in as Charlie's date at his sister's wedding in an attempt to keep Rory away. They'd had a secret relationship because Rory was in the closet, and he had subsequently broken things off, but it seemed Rory had wanted to use the wedding as an excuse to get closer to Charlie again.

The ploy had worked in a wonderful way for Kris and Charlie.

Rory had kept away after that, and from the tight hug Connor was giving him, it seemed he'd stayed away.

I didn't hear their first exchange of words but also didn't miss how tense Rory became when I stretched my hand out to him. He shook it but didn't look at me. He was probably worried I'd give his secret away.

He didn't need to worry because despite my dislike for the guy, I wasn't an ass, and there was no way I'd ever out someone. Not that he needed to know that, hence the slight smile on my lips as I greeted him.

I noticed Charlie took advantage of my presence to get back to Kris.

"How are you doing?" I asked as Rory let go of my hand and took a step back.

"Um... good, thanks. James, right?"

I nodded as Connor sent me a puzzled look and focused back on his friend.

"Are you here to stay?" Connor asked.

Rory looked unsure about my presence, but I didn't move an inch, so he turned to Connor.

"Yeah, I think so."

"Oh man, that's awesome," Connor said beaming. "It'll be great to have you back. It's been shit in the last year without you."

Rory smiled back at Connor and nodded. "It's nice to be back. I hope it's okay that I barged in unannounced."

"What the fuck, man. You know you're always welcome here. Come on, let's get you some beer and a cremated burger," Connor said, placing his arm around Rory's shoulders and guiding him to the grill where his dad and uncle were handing out all the food.

I was left staring at Connor and Rory as they moved away. Suddenly, the soda I had in my hand tasted as flat as I felt as I watched the two friends catching up.

Connor's dad greeted Rory with a hug, and his mom fussed over him as if he was a long-lost child returning home.

"Do we need to have the big brother conversation?" Kris asked as he approached me with a fresh drink.

Earlier, we'd been talking about Kris and Charlie's plans to return to Lydovia in a few days while keeping an eye on Connor without seeming too obvious about it. It seemed I'd failed miserably if his comment was anything to go by.

"What do you mean?"

He raised a brow. "My friend, I've known you for years, and I've never seen you struggle to keep your eyes away from anything as much as you're trying with Connor. What's going on?"

"Nothing," I said, trying to keep the jealousy from my voice.

"Right, right. Same nothing as that time when you had a crush on Professor Robertson and were convinced he was into you until you saw his wife picking him up after class? That kind of nothing?"

"If you weren't my boss, I'd punch you right now," I said with a laugh.

"Never stopped you before."

"Don't tempt me."

"What's up, guys?" Charlie said, walking into Kris's arms with his sketchpad in hand.

"Nothing much, baby. Are you okay with Rory being here?" Kris asked.

"Yeah, he doesn't bother me anymore," Charlie said, looking over at Rory. "He doesn't look okay though."

"And this is why I love you, Charlie. Even now, you're still worried about someone who wasn't good to you."

Kris tilted Charlie's head up and placed a small kiss on his lips. I looked away and back to Rory. Maybe Charlie was right. Even though he smiled and engaged in conversation with people around him, I noticed how he would shrink into himself when he didn't think anyone was looking.

Every so often, he'd look at Connor. Was that longing in his eyes? Was Rory in love with Connor?

"Where has he been? Connor hasn't mentioned him once," I asked.

"Singapore. He got a job there shortly after Hannah's wedding last year. I don't think he's been back since," Charlie replied. "Maybe it'll be good for Connor to have his best friend back."

I stilled at Charlie's comment and then chastised myself for it because he noticed.

"I'm sorry, James."

"That's okay, I know what you mean. They have been friends for longer than we ever were. I'm going to do a perimeter check," I said before I walked out through the back gate, placing my old drink and the new one I'd grabbed earlier on a nearby table.

Kris and Charlie always kept a low profile when in Chester Falls. They didn't hire fancy cars or paraded around town. Mostly, they spent time with Charlie's family, so these perimeter checks were more to satisfy my own need to know the whole family was safe and there wasn't anyone lurking around the property.

"I'm calling bullshit," the voice said from behind me.

"You know, the purpose of a perimeter check is to make sure you, your fiancé, and his family are safe. If you're with me, it kinda defeats the purpose."

"James, you're my head of security, but above everything, you're my friend," Kris said. "I'm failing to see any paparazzi, so are you going to tell me why you ran out of there after that conversation?"

I shook my head and leaned against the tall wooden fence.

"I'll make this easy on you by calling out that I can see you have feelings for him."

"Your sister is rubbing off on you," I chuckled. Aleks was only months away from getting married and being crowned queen of Lydovia while their father took a step back in his royal duties. She was not only the most down to earth but also the most perceptive person I'd ever met. It seemed that the skill ran in the family.

He punched my arm lightly. "I'll tell her you said that. She'll be happy."

"Do you remember that time at college when I got stupidly drunk?" I asked.

"Which one?" he laughed.

"Fuck you. It happened once," I said, raising a finger.

"Sure, sure...carry on."

"Do you remember when I told you that the reason I couldn't get a boyfriend was because I was in love?"

Kris gasped and stared at me. His eyes were full of something that looked a lot like pity to me.

"I met Connor at a time when I was finding out about my sexuality and that I was attracted to boys. He was a great person and a good friend, and he was so gorgeous even then." I smiled thinking back to a time when Connor was all height, muscles, and floppy copper hair. "I didn't know how to tell when another boy liked me, so I made a mistake."

"What happened?" Kris asked.

"I kissed him and he ran. That was the day my mom took us away."

Kris looked at me like everything suddenly made sense to him, so I confirmed it.

"Last year was the first time I saw him in fifteen years."

"And all those feelings came back?"

I nodded.

"But he's straight, right?" Kris asked, although he didn't sound too sure himself.

"We kissed last night. God, Kris, it was the best experience of my entire life, and if I was to die today, I'd die happy with that memory alone, but..."

"You want more?" Kris guessed.

"Yeah."

"So what's the problem?"

"He's confused about what happened, and now Rory's here."

I carried on walking around the property, knowing Kris wouldn't let it go even though I was more than ready to put this conversation to bed.

"What does Rory have to do with it?"

"Doesn't matter. I'm going to fly back to Lydovia with you

this week. Tomorrow, I will catch up with officer LaCruz about the investigation, and if necessary, Ryan can stay behind with Connor."

Kris held my elbow to stop me, but I pulled it back.

"I have meetings to attend in order to go through all the security arrangements for Aleks's wedding."

I turned around when I heard Kris laughing.

"What?"

"You are answering to Charlie if you think it's going to be that easy to let go of your assignment. And I can tell you from experience with that one particular William's boy, they're not easy to let go of either."

CONNOR

"Hey, Sweetie pie," I said, picking up Bubbles from her sunning spot under the UV lamp and placing her on my chest as I lay down on the floor with one of the sofa cushions under my head.

This was one of my favorite things to do, and she seemed to enjoy it, too, especially because I had her favorite treats in my hand.

I let her do her usual circular crawl over my chest before she settled in the middle waiting for her dried shrimp.

"I'm not going to judge you on your choice of food, but this stinks, Bubbles."

She swallowed her food and raised her head asking for a little rub. I obliged, as always. She'd had a less than ideal start in life after being abandoned on the side of the road, and I would do everything I could to keep her happy and healthy. Even if she was a little escape artist that loved to keep me on my toes...or bite them.

"Uncle Rory came home. Did you know that? Yeah. I think there's something going on with him, but I'm sure he'll tell me when he's ready. Maybe he can visit us when we're back home. Would you like that?"

Bubbles opened her little beak as if she was agreeing with me. That, or she just wanted another shrimp.

Anyone finding me having a one-way conversation with a turtle would laugh, but Bubbles had gotten me through a lot of tough times in the last year when I felt lonely, not only when I had to make tough decisions at work but also when something was good. In some ways, she knew more about me than anyone else in my life.

"Did you see that kiss yesterday? It was hot, right?"

She bumped her head against my hand so I scratched her carapace lightly, watching as she closed her eyes and looked like she was enjoying being spoiled.

"What do I do, Bubbles? I haven't got a clue about being with a man."

I didn't mind so much being labeled as gay or bi. Growing up with two LGBT siblings, I knew I'd be supported no matter who I happened to be with, but how was it possible that up until now, I hadn't ever felt attraction for another guy?

"What if I try to take it further and I don't like it? What if I'm no good at it?"

Bubbles stared at me with her little but big-for-her-face eyes.

"Don't look at me like that. I know you're a turtle and you can't help. Jeez, have another shrimp, and this is the last one."

I heard the front door unlock, and a moment later, James stood under the archway that separated the living area from the bedrooms and hallway.

"Hey, everything okay next door? Did Ryan have a good day off?"

I hadn't seen much of James after Rory turned up this afternoon, and I hadn't had a chance to talk to him because as soon as we came back to the apartment, he said he had to see Ryan.

"Yeah, he went to visit a friend in Fairfield."

"Good, sounds nice."

There was something about the way James stood that put me

on edge. I placed Bubbles back inside her tank and went over to the kitchen sink to wash my hands.

"I'm going back to Lydovia with Charlie and Kris. Ryan will stay here with you."

"You're leaving." I gripped the tea towel and hoped my voice sounded steadier than I felt as I stated the obvious.

"I have work to do out there and Ryan is more than capable."

The way he said it felt both like a dismissal of what had happened last night and the assumption that I was some kind of damsel in distress that needed guarding.

"I am more than capable of looking after myself. I've let you take over in the last few days to pacify my brother, but that was it. I'm going back to work tomorrow and then I'll go back to my house, where I belong."

He called my name as I walked past him, but I ignored him and went straight to my room.

I closed the door quietly behind me when I really wanted to slam it, but I'd be damned if I was going to show any emotion.

My head throbbed and my body ached as if I'd been run over by a truck. Even the gentle touch of the nurse as she cleaned and dressed the cut on my face was adding to my brain fog.

"Do you have anyone that can pick you up and take you home?" she asked.

"I'll take a cab."

"No need. I'll take you home," Ryan said, pushing aside the curtain of the treatment area.

"Sir, unless you're family, you can't be here," the nurse said before looking at me.

"It's okay. He's a close friend," I said. Well, it was the best I could do to avoid any problems.

"Ryan, thank you for coming, but I'll be going home as soon as I'm discharged. I will take a cab."

His jaw was locked tight as if he was stopping himself from saying something, but I wasn't standing down. "Goodbye, Ryan."

He stood there for a few seconds before leaving, which was when I allowed myself to take a deep breath.

"I'm all done here, but you have to wait for the result of the scan. Why don't you lay back and try to rest?"

"Thanks," I said, taking her advice. I looked at my phone briefly and saw there was only one message from my boss asking me when I'd be back at work before putting it back in my pocket without replying.

I closed my eyes, willing the headache away. This morning I'd packed my clothes and left the apartment with the intention of going back after work to pick up Bubbles and then head back to my own home.

A stupid accident at work was now putting my plan at risk, because if it turned out I had a concussion, I was going to need to stay with someone. Maybe I could call Aunt Gina and stay with her.

I didn't want to worry my parents, and Charlie and Kris were about to travel back to Lydovia. The last thing I wanted was to have them change their plans for me. That was also the last thought I had before I must have fallen asleep, because when I came to, there was a warm, heavy weight holding one of my hands down.

Surprisingly, despite still feeling a little dizzy, my headache had subsided. Even more surprising was seeing James sitting on a plastic chair that looked like it could barely take his weight, holding my hands so tight as if there was a chance of me letting go.

His head was resting on his hands, hence the heavy weight, and his short, dirty blond hair looked a little longer than it had been just days ago when I first saw him at the cave.

"Hey," I said gently. I wasn't sure if he was asleep and didn't want to startle him.

His head shot up, but he didn't let go of my hands.

"Fuck, Connor, you scared me to death."

"Why?"

I moved my hands so he'd let them go, but he only relaxed his hold a little bit.

"Why? Why do you think? First of all, you packed all your things and left the apartment this morning before Ryan could take you to work, and then I got a call from him to say you're in the hospital." James finally let go of my hands to run his own over his face and through his hair.

"It was only an accident. It could have happened any time, so why would I call anyone?" I asked. For some reason, I was feeling strangely calm. Maybe the pills I'd been given earlier for my headache were better than I thought. I smiled at that.

"Tell me what happened," James said, shifting in his chair to sit closer.

"I was at work and had to file some paperwork. The filing cabinet was loose on the wall, so it fell on me and knocked me out. All I got was a scratch on my face, that's all," I said, trying to pacify him.

"Actually, Mr. Williams, that's not entirely true." A man wearing light green scrubs said coming inside my room. "I'm Dr. Patel. I'm afraid you have a mild concussion."

I groaned at the news. This was exactly the opposite of what I was hoping for.

"When can I go home?" I asked.

"You can be discharged if you follow these instructions and you aren't on your own for the next few days."

He handed me a piece of paper, which James took from my hands and started reading.

I sighed. "I take it you're not here to give me a ride home," I said.

"Not on your life, Connor Williams. You're coming with me back to the apartment, and you're going to stay in bed for the next week."

I hated my stupid dick for reading something else in the

words he'd said instead of what they really meant, which was that I was going to be under house arrest.

"Besides," he said, ignoring my inner turmoil. "Princess Bubbles has been in a mood all day because she misses you."

Now that did put a smile on my face.

JAMES

It didn't matter that his smile had been brought on by me mentioning Bubbles. After how we left things last night, the fact Connor wasn't shutting me down completely felt like a victory.

I helped him out of the gurney and onto his feet. He was a little unsteady at first but managed to do it mostly on his own.

"Sorry," he said. "Head feels a little fuzzy."

"It's okay. Let's get you in the wheelchair and out to the car."

My heart rate still hadn't quite recovered from when I'd received the call from Ryan to come to the small Falls Memorial Hospital. I was just glad it had been a five-minute drive rather than the thirty it would have taken to get to New Haven.

I'd spent part of the morning in conference calls with my team back in Lydovia while Kris and Charlie had packed their stuff, and then I'd taken them back to their new house. I'd run through the list of security requirements I'd started with Ryan while the happy couple had gone around discussing renovations.

All day, I'd found myself with my fingers hovering over the text message app on my phone wanting to check up on Connor but then forcing myself to focus on my work and let Ryan do his job.

It was all pointless because as soon as I'd seen Connor on that gurney with his eyes closed and a cut on his face covered with butterfly bandages, I knew there was no way I'd be getting on that airplane back to Lydovia tomorrow. I'd sent Ryan a text to tell him of the change of plan, to which he'd replied straight away saying he was already packed.

"Can I see Bubbles?" Connor asked as soon as we arrived at the apartment.

"You probably need to get some rest," I said.

"Please, just for a little bit. I'll sit on the sofa."

He looked tired, but he seemed fairly steady on his feet. His whole face lit up when I placed Bubbles on his hand.

"Hey Baby girl," he said scratching her tiny neck. She stretched up in delight, closing her little eyes.

"Does she know she's not a cat?" I chuckled.

Connor laughed "She does seem to be as stealthy."

"Do you want something to eat?" I asked.

"No, thanks. I'll just go to bed now, if that's okay," he said stifling a yawn.

With Bubbles settled back in her tank with a big lettuce leaf, I helped Connor back to his room.

I left him to undress while I went back to the kitchen to grab him a glass of water and then nearly dropped it when I came back to the room and saw the bruises on his arms and chest.

He was sitting in bed with the covers pulled up to his waist, his hand running over the various dark purple marks.

"Sorry, I know it looks awful. Who knew filing cabinets were so heavy. So much for putting in some extra hours at the start of the day." He laughed, but I could see the tension in his body.

I sat on the bed next to him and took his hands in mine.

"Hey, are you okay?"

He shook his head. "There was a loud bang and then one of the cabinets was on the floor. When I stepped away, the other one fell on me. I thought I was going to be crushed." His voice broke a little, and I placed my hand on the side of his face that had the band-aids and tilted his head a little, rubbing my thumb over the uninjured skin and jaw.

"I've lived through many close calls, but getting that call from Ryan telling me to go to the hospital was..." I couldn't finish my thought because it was too painful to consider what might have happened. "It doesn't matter."

"I'm sorry I left so early this morning," he said looking down again. "I didn't mean to run out on Ryan."

"Yes, you did," I said, giving him a pointed look.

Connor must have heard the humor in my voice because he did look up then and smiled.

"Okay, maybe I did."

He leaned his head back against the headboard and closed his eyes. I watched him for a moment, his chest rising and falling with every breath, his beautiful face that even with a cut and bandages was still the most striking I'd ever seen, and those damned cute freckles of his.

I moved to get up when he opened his eyes, and then his hand gripped mine.

"Will you stay with me?"

I wasn't sure if he meant for a while, the night, or forever, but it didn't matter because between his bright green eyes looking at me full of vulnerability and my stupid heart, there wasn't a chance of the answer being anything other than yes.

One week of waking up with Connor plastered to my body and I was wound up so tight I was afraid of what would happen when I finally snapped.

After bringing Connor home from the hospital, I'd spent the first two days monitoring his concussion closely, waking him up every few hours, asking him questions, and checking for anything that was different in his behavior.

Charlie and Kris had delayed their return home, but when

they realized Connor was recovering well, they agreed they should go back to Lydovia, especially as Charlie had a public engagement where he was opening an art gallery dedicated to showcasing younger artists.

In those two days, Connor had become increasingly frustrated with the lack of sleep and the fact I insisted he stayed in bed resting. As soon as I let him sleep the whole night, his mood improved drastically.

Mine, however, was hanging on by a thread because that first night Connor asked me to sleep with him in his bed wasn't the only time. He'd asked me again every single night.

The first night, I'd slept fully dressed until I had a chance to go to Mason's General Store to buy a couple of sets of pajamas since I normally slept in my underwear, and there was no way I'd risk that around Connor.

The third night, I woke up with Connor holding my hands. We'd been facing each other, and his hands were around mine as though he was afraid I'd leave. With each subsequent night, he kept getting closer and closer, meaning I was getting less and less sleep.

I was terrified he'd notice my body's reaction to his and would freak out. Despite my lack of any decent sleep, I couldn't deny I'd enjoyed all those hours I'd spent watching him.

Those little sounds he made as he'd sometimes call out for Bubbles, his brother and sister, and my favorite, when he called out for me.

Sometimes he'd giggle at whatever he was dreaming of, and with each passing minute, I was losing my heart to him all over again.

I sighed, knowing I needed to move just like I'd done every morning before Connor woke up.

"What's up?" he asked in a sleep-filled voice.

I was laying on my back, so I turned to face him and opened my eyes slowly, afraid of what I'd see in his.

"You're...um...I can't move."

"Is that so bad?" he asked, his hand moving from where it had been resting on my chest up to touch my lips.

"No," I whispered. "But—"

"I want to kiss you again, James," he whispered back, his fingers tracing my lips gently.

"You need to be absolutely sure you want it, Connor, because I don't know if I can handle—" My words were interrupted by his mouth on mine.

This wasn't a slow, tentative, shy, and uncertain kiss. Connor's hand slid to the back of my neck, keeping me from breaking the moment. As if I would.

I was finally where I'd wanted to be since I was fifteen years old, in Connor's arms, tasting his lips, and finally feeling like I was home.

My body responded to the kiss like a fire responded to oxygen.

"Connor," I gasped.

"Please, James."

I was afraid to ask what he wanted in case there was a chance we weren't on the same page, but then he moved. He fucking moved and suddenly everything was Connor, his body, his smell, and his very hard cock rubbing up against mine.

"Oh fuck, I'm so glad," I said between kissing him and exploring his body with my hands.

He chuckled. "Why are you glad?"

"Nevermind, just kiss me some more."

The way things were going, I was going to come in my pajamas in two minutes flat. I had to slow things down a little so I hooked my leg around him and turned us over so I could lay on top of him using my knees to put some space between us.

His eyes opened wide, and for a moment, I wondered if the change of position was too much too soon, but Connor wrapped his legs around me and pulled me closer.

I grabbed his hands, interlacing our fingers above his head, kissing him again. With very little to hold me up, I ended up pressing my whole weight down on him. He groaned, a sound that vibrated all the way down my body.

"So good, James, fuck...so goo—"

"FUUCK!" I screamed in pain as my little finger was once again the victim of the family hooligan.

Fucking turtle.

CONNOR

"What the hell, Bubbles," James squealed.

He raised his hand, showing my cock-blocking turtle hanging on to his little finger. The move caused his body to press further onto mine. I groaned from the feeling and immediately imagined how it would be if there were no clothes between us.

James moved to my side, unaware of the thoughts coursing through my head.

I'd been once or twice on the receiving end of one of Bubbles' bites and knew how painful they could be, so I wasn't surprised to see his attention remain on Princess Bite-a-Lot.

I reached for her to help release his finger, and as soon as I held her, she let go, so I placed her on my chest.

"She was trying to protect me from the big bad man on top of me," I said.

James's dimpled smile lit up the room more than the light of the morning sun coming through the curtains.

"Bubbles, we've had this conversation already, haven't we?" James said, his eyes on my pet who admittedly almost looked embarrassed with her little head bowed down. "You can't just interrupt a guy when he's about to get lucky."

I chuckled. "Oh, I didn't realize I was a sure thing."

James looked down at my still hard cock tenting my boxer shorts and raised a brow.

"Is this really happening?" he asked. Some of the heat from the heavy make out session was still there in his big hazel eyes, but there was also a tiny speck of doubt.

I nodded. "Yes, if you want to, this is very much, totally, one-hundred percent happening." I stretched up my neck to kiss him since one of my hands was trapped under him and the other was stroking Bubbles.

"What made you change your mind?"

"I didn't need my mind changing. I just needed to understand how I felt." The room was slowly filling up with light from the morning sun. Somehow, this moment, with Bubbles on me and James by my side, was the perfect time to do this. "That kiss when we were fifteen. That changed me, James."

His eyes flitted between mine. "But you ran away."

"That may have been the first of the many idiotic decisions I've made in my life, but maybe it was for the best."

James stilled at my comment and looked away, but I pulled him back to me by releasing Bubbles and cradling his face with my hand.

"Don't. Let me explain. If I'd stayed and we kissed some more, what would have happened? You would still have left the next day, and I would have been more confused and upset."

He turned his head and kissed the palm of my hand. His hand was on my chest, rubbing soft circles and keeping Bubbles in place.

"I know. You're right," he said.

"Why don't you take Princess Bite-a-Lot back to her castle," I said and then raised my head again for another kiss. "If you happen to lose your clothes on the way back, I won't be too upset."

In the race between the hare and the turtle, my heart was definitely the hare with how fast it was beating. And somehow, coming last didn't seem like a bad thing either.

While James was out of the room, I went to the bathroom to wash my hands and then removed my clothes before I got back in bed, wondering how I'd got here.

I'd been building up the courage to kiss James all week. At first, I didn't know if he'd want me to kiss him again, but then I felt how his body reacted to mine every night as he slept beside me.

We'd always fallen asleep on our sides of the bed, but somehow, I seemed to gravitate toward him as the night went on. I'd accepted that as my body's way of telling my mind what it craved.

Even when I woke up to find myself glued to James, I couldn't move away. I'd even dared to touch his face and feel how soft his skin was because he always shaved before he came to bed.

Of course, he'd be gone before I got up despite my best attempts to ensure he stayed put.

A whole week of anticipation of waking up with him and hoping he'd let me try again, and today, it had finally happened. Maybe I was rested enough that I'd naturally woken up earlier, or maybe I'd caught him in that moment before he made the decision to leave the bed.

Either way, it didn't matter. I'd had my chance, and boy, was I going to take it. When James had turned us over, I had a slight moment of panic when I didn't know what was expected of me, but one look into his hazel eyes and I realized I didn't need to know.

Deep down, I knew James would never do anything to hurt me. The fact he'd left my bed every morning to avoid any awkward moments told me everything I needed to know.

"Fuck me," James gasped from the bedroom door.

His eyes looked me up and down, pausing when they got to my hand. The hand that was slowly and teasingly stroking my cock.

"Maybe not today," I said in a gravelly voice. "But I'd like that."

As requested, James had divested himself from his pajamas, but he'd kept his boxer shorts on. He came over but stopped at the side of the bed when I raised my hand.

"You're gorgeous, James. God, how did I not jump you a year ago when I saw you?"

His body was like a piece of Greek sculpture. There were muscles and beautiful tan skin as far as my eager eye could see. He had a pair of wings tattooed on his chest. I hadn't seen them before and wondered if they meant something to him, or even if he had any other tattoos.

"I honestly don't know," he said, his cocky voice making my cock harden even more in my hand.

"Come here," I said, holding out my hand. James wavered for a nanosecond, but then he removed his boxer shorts and hovered his body tentatively over mine until I removed my hand from my cock and pulled him down to me by his waist.

We both hissed when our hard cocks lined up, the friction causing my whole body to tremble like there were millions of tiny explosions of pleasure going off everywhere. Fuck, if it was like this and we hadn't even got to the sex part yet, I was sure to die from my impending orgasm.

"Can I suck you?" James asked.

"Fuck, yes," I said before I kissed him, making sure my tongue memorized the taste and feel of his.

"Are you su—"

I put both my hands on his face to force him to look at me in the eyes.

"If you ask me one more time if I'm sure about this, I'm going to flip you over and take your cock in my mouth right the fuck now. My cock is leaking like a faucet because of how good it feels against yours. I may have never been with a man, but I'm not a fucking virgin, James."

My words must have settled something in James because he

kissed me like the entrance to my soul was in my mouth, and his hands roamed my body as if they were trying to settle all those tiny explosions. They weren't, they were making it worse. My whole body was on fucking fire.

"Please, James. I'm not going to last. Just do it already," I said as I gasped for air.

"God, you turn me on so much. I don't even know where to start with you."

"My cock, James, my fucking cock."

He laughed. "I love this demanding Connor."

I didn't have any time to consider the words he'd just said before my cock was surrounded by wet heat and pressure. One look down at James and I had to lean my head back on the pillow because it was too much.

"Look at me, Connor," he demanded. "Look how hard you are for me, baby."

I shook my head because I couldn't do anything else. It felt as though my whole self, my living cells and my soul, were congregating inside Jame's mouth, so I was incapable of any coherent speech or any kind of brain function.

The pressure on my lower back built up slowly, and I knew it wouldn't take long to give James the orgasm he'd been drawing out of me for what felt like hours but in reality was probably only a couple of minutes.

Suddenly, as I thought I was about to come, everything came to a halt. I looked down again to see James holding my balls to stop me from coming, and he wasn't sucking me anymore. Instead, he was kissing my inner thighs while his other hand was slowly moving down over my balls, to the one place I'd never considered before in any sexual encounter.

JAMES

I chuckled at Connor's frustrated-slash-murderous look but continued my exploration of his creamy white skin. He always used to be so tan when we were young, but I guessed he now spent more time indoors at work than he did outdoors.

"Sorry, baby, it wasn't your orgasm I was trying to stop, it was mine," I said, peppering his thighs with small kisses and making my way down

"Exactly! Do I need to explain to you the purpose of an orgasm? Or are you just trying to kill us both?" Connor said, and when I looked at him, his lips had an adorable pout I just had to kiss.

"Not trying to kill you, but I don't want this to stop either," I confessed.

Connor hooked his leg over me and the undulating move of his hips trapped our cocks together in a way that got me back to where I'd been before I stopped our climax.

"You know," he said, looking at the clock on the wall, "you're allowed more than one orgasm per day. In fact, I'd say in the interest of public safety, you should have at least two."

"Oh really? Public safety?"

"Yeah, you get grumpy too easily," he teased before he slapped my ass.

I gave his mouth a bruising kiss that promised what I was about to deliver and then made my way back down his body.

This time there was no teasing or going slow. I took Connor's cock to the back of my throat like a thirsty man having his first sip of water in weeks. Connor moaned and raised his hips up to meet my hungry mouth every time I let up a little.

When he put his hand on my head and threaded his fingers through my short hair, I felt owned. I swallowed around the head of his cock and only had enough time to draw a short breath through my nose before Connor shouted out his orgasm and I felt the warm, salty taste of his release.

My own orgasm built up in my spine, and I barely had enough time to stroke myself to finish over Connor's taut stomach and then collapse on top of him.

"Fuck, Con. That was incredible," I said, taking his mouth again. I was never going to get tired of his mouth, and fuck if he wasn't the best kisser.

I didn't even consider that he was trying his cum for the first time because I'd been so lost in my own head. When I tried to pull out of his mouth, he kissed me deeper.

"Like I said," Connor stated as if he could read my thoughts. "I'm not a virgin."

The thought that Connor had tasted himself before made my spent cock twitch a little.

"Let me clean you up," I said, making a move to get my heavy weight off of him.

"I like being dirty with you." He ran his hand over my release that was smeared all over his stomach and then put his finger in his mouth. "Hmm, you taste nicer than me."

I laid on my back and stared at the ceiling. "You're gonna fucking kill me, Connor Williams."

Sex had never been like this for me. It had been a means to an end, and even when I'd been in a relationship, I'd never felt this way.

There had been this rush to get closer, to get to know each other's bodies for the first time. But then there was this incredible chemistry between us that allowed time for fun, to tease each other and laugh. When did I ever laugh during sex, in a good way?

"A dime for your thoughts," he said, bumping his elbow against mine.

"No thoughts. I'm dead."

He laughed and then straddled me, kissing me again. "I thought you'd sucked my brains out through my cock...but it seems there's still some left."

I looked down, and sure enough, his cock was filling again.

"Come on, let's take a shower before you kill me for real. How about we get out to get some fresh air? I think it's safe to say you're all recovered from your concussion."

"Could we go to my place? I'd like to get all the broken stuff out of there."

I would have expected him to be upset at doing something like that, but he seemed okay, so I nodded and then put my arms around his waist as I sat up and then carried him to the bathroom and into the shower.

Our shower took a little longer than anticipated, so we didn't leave the apartment until it was close to lunchtime.

"Do you want to share a stack of pancakes from Benny's before we go?" I asked. "You've worn me out, and now I'm starving."

"I'll never say no to Momma Ruth's pancakes."

The sun was out, but it was still chilly enough to require a coat, which was the reason I even noticed the barefoot man kneeling down by the flower beds wearing nothing else but a t-shirt and overalls as we made our way to the diner.

"Hey, Olly, how's it going?" Connor asked the man.

"Oh hi, Connor. Never better. Summer is here, and my flowers are loving it. Who's your friend?"

"This is James." Connor pointed at me and then said, "And this is Oleander, but we call him Olly. Olly looks after all of the flowers in town."

"Must keep you busy," I said, extending my hand to greet him. The man had the friendliest smile, and I couldn't help but feel drawn into it.

"I wouldn't have it any other way. I know all the flowers in Chester Falls, and trust me, they all have their own little quirks." He giggled as if we were in on his joke before he pulled a little bag from the wooden crate with his gardening tools and gave it to Connor.

"What's this?" he asked.

"Lilac seeds. They'll take a little while to flower, so you have to think carefully where you're going to plant them. Like many things in life, getting them is easy, but protecting them so they grow healthy and happy is a little harder but well worth the effort."

Something told me Olly wasn't talking about the flowers when his eyes met mine as he handed Connor the small bag.

"Thanks, Olly. See you around."

"Bye-bye, boys," he said, going back to his flowers and ignoring our raised hands as we waved goodbye.

Once we'd replenished our energy levels with coffee and pancakes, we drove over to Connor's house. I looked at Connor to assess his mood once I parked in the driveway.

"I'm not sure how I'm supposed to feel right now," he said.

"How do you feel?"

"Not like I'm coming home. I feel like I'm just pulling up to someone else's house."

Connor opened the car door but stopped when I put my hand on his arm.

"You're the one with the Psychology degree, but I bet that once you have your new furniture here, this will feel like your home again. Shall we go in?"

He nodded and exited the car.

There was a little pile of letters behind the front door, so I walked past Connor as he picked them up and then he joined me in the kitchen. A shiver ran down my spine as if my instincts were telling me something wasn't right.

I took my gun from the holster and asked Connor to stay in the kitchen while I checked the rest of the house. It was likely that if someone was in the house, they'd have left as we arrived, but my instincts were on high alert, and I didn't like it one bit.

The sound of something dropping in the kitchen got me running back to Connor.

I found him by the sink. The mug he'd been about to fill up with water was in the sink, fortunately still in one piece, but Connor was shaking like a leaf.

"What's up?" I asked, turning the tap off.

Connor gave me the contents of the letter he had in his hand. The envelope didn't have a stamp. I wanted to laugh at the newspaper cutouts that formed the message for how cliché it was, but the message itself was to be taken seriously.

You ruined my life and now I'm going to ruin yours.

I looked at Connor, and all color had drained from his face.

"Was there anything else in the envelope?"

Connor gave me a photo of Charlie and Kris taken at the gym when they'd been climbing. I knew it was a recent photo because Ryan was right next to them.

I pulled up my phone and dialed Ryan's number.

"Hey, boss, sick of your holiday yet?" Ryan said on the other side of the line.

"Ryan, do you remember taking Kris and Charlie to the climbing wall?"

"Yeah, why?"

"Was there anyone in the hall with you?"

"A kid, Brad. I asked Kris if he wanted me to clear the hall, but they knew him from last year and said he was a good kid. Is there a problem?"

I didn't have a chance to answer because an explosion by the back door of the kitchen threw me onto the floor.

CONNOR

One moment I had my eyes locked on James as he tried to find out more information about the photo, and the next I was on the floor with him on top of me, my ears ringing from the loud bang.

There was no time to think or ask questions. James crouched down behind the kitchen island and pulled me with him, picking up the letter and photograph and putting it in his pocket.

"Was that a bomb?" I asked.

"No, it was a stun grenade. Stay behind me."

He stayed low, crawling on the floor, and I followed behind him. The front door wasn't far, but we didn't have time to get to it when another grenade smashed through the window and landed on the floor.

"Fuck!" James shouted and put his arms around me, guiding me to my room at the end of the hall.

As soon as I was inside, he pushed me so hard I went over the bed and landed on the floor on the other side. James hadn't yet closed the door behind him when the grenade went off, except this time, it wasn't just the noise and a flash of light.

The windows in my bedroom shattered mere feet away from

me. I looked over the ripped mattress, and where my door had been, but now there was just part of a missing wall.

"James!" I shouted.

I didn't give him time to reply before I crawled around the bed to find him. Somehow, despite having nearly flown over half the length of my bedroom, I hadn't hurt myself.

Smoke started filling the room as I came around the bed to find James knocked out and with a bleeding cut on his head.

"No! No, James, you can't do this to me." I didn't know if I could touch him or how hurt he was, but the smoke was getting thicker, and there was heat coming from the corridor.

We needed to get out of the house right now. What if there were more of those grenades?

I turned him on his side and cleaned the trickle of blood from his face using the bedsheet hanging off the bed that had been cut up during the break-in.

"James, please wake up, baby. I need you to help me get you out of here."

Tears filled my eyes. I got up and opened the window, clearing any glass from the ledge.

I managed to drag James over to the window, but I had no clue how I'd get him over to the other side.

"James, baby..." I said holding him close to me, kissing the side of his head.

A hand touched mine, and I would have sobbed in relief if I hadn't gone straight into survival mode.

"James, thank god."

"We need to get out," he said groggily, getting on his hands and knees.

"Can you get up through the window?" I pulled up a chair to help us up, and shortly we were outside the house.

We held each other up and walked away from the house. Police sirens rang in the distance. Hopefully, one of my neighbors had called them when they heard the loud explosion.

As soon as we reached the other side of the street, we

collapsed on my neighbors' lawn. James's hands were everywhere on me.

"I'm okay, I'm okay. How are you feeling?" I asked, tilting his head to look at the small cut on his forehead. It had finally stopped bleeding.

"I'm okay," James said, taking a deep breath and sitting back on the grass. He gasped when he looked up.

I turned around to see my house engulfed in flames. It was a good thing I was sitting down because I wouldn't have been able to stay upright at the sight of my home falling apart in front of my very eyes.

"Why is this happening?" I cried.

"I don't know, baby. But we'll figure it out."

His arms around me were the only thing keeping me from breaking down completely.

"Oh my lord, oh goodness. Are you alright? Joanie, my neighbor yelled as she came running out of her house with her husband Bill right on her heels.

"Let me get you boys some water. We called the fire department for you."

"Thanks, Bill," I said.

"Honey can you bring my first aid box too?" she asked Bill.

Joanie kneeled on the grass in front of James and looked at his cut. Bill came back a moment later with two bottles of water and handed his wife a small box. In a few dexterous movements, James had his head cleaned and bandaged.

"They should be here any moment now, boys. We called them as soon as we heard the first bang. What on our lord's earth was that noise?" Joanie asked.

"Probably a gas bottle, right boys?" Bill said, and I could tell from his expression he didn't want Joanie to worry that it could be something more.

"Yes, that's right, Bill. I have a camping stove somewhere in the house."

"Bill," James said. "Did you notice anything strange recently?

Or did you see anyone coming over to Connor's house? Like salesmen or people knocking on the door, maybe while you were out gardening?"

Joanie and Bill looked at each other.

"About a week ago we saw someone delivering some mail to your house. I thought it was strange because the mailman had been. We were waiting on a package and ended up having a chat with him. Nice chap."

I looked at James while Joanie rambled about the mailman. He looked like he was trying to figure something out.

"And you haven't seen anyone since?" he asked.

"I thought I saw someone on the side of the house two days ago by the fence. I went to check it out because your car wasn't in the driveway, and I didn't want you to have someone breaking in, but by the time I got there, I didn't see anyone."

"Thanks, Bill," I said as the loud sirens turning the corner of the street became too loud to hold a conversation.

There was nothing we could do but watch as the firemen tried to contain the flames, but I suspected there wouldn't be much left of my house.

A police car was right behind the fire trucks, and they parked along the curb in front of us. I was happy to see Scott in the driver's seat, but my heart sank when I noticed my sister right next to him.

She flew out of the car and came straight to us.

"What the fuck happened? Are you okay?"

Her pink hair was in a long plait with loose strands all over. She'd either had a hard day at work or this was induced by the news of my house being on fire.

"We're okay, Hannah. Calm down," I said, pulling her down to my level for a hug.

"What happened?"

Scott, who'd been speaking to the fireman in charge, came over to us. I waited until he was within earshot before I told them what happened.

"We came here to start clearing up all the stuff damaged from the break-in. Someone threw in a noise bomb—"

"Stun grenade," James clarified for Scott's notes.

"We tried to leave, but then there was another one that busted through the window, except that was a real one."

"How did you get out?" Scott asked.

"The grenade blasted out the windows. We got out through the one in Connor's bedroom," James explained.

"Are you up for a full statement back at the station?" Scott asked.

Both James and I nodded and then James handed Scott the letter.

"What's this?"

"We'd just found that when the stun grenade went off," I said.

"Hannah, where are your parents?" Scott asked.

"At my aunt and uncle's. Why? What's wrong?" she asked.

"Looks like there's more behind the break-in than we thought, but this could be a good sign. This guy here is looking at the camera, who is he?" Scott asked.

"That's Ryan, he was with Kris and Charlie that day. I was on the phone with him when the grenade came in. Ryan said there was only one person in the climbing area at the time, a kid called Brad. Apparently, he works at the rec center." James said.

"He could be the one who took that photo or at least may know more. I'm going to stop over at the gym to see my buddy Mac and get a feel for this guy. Can you meet me at the station later?" Scott said.

"Sure, we're stuck here until the fire truck moves anyway. My car is in the driveway." All I could think was I was glad I'd parked far enough away from the house that the car should be okay.

I didn't even realize I'd leaned against James until I felt his arms wrap around me. He nuzzled my neck and whispered in my ear. "Everything's gonna be okay, baby. I promise."

Hannah was grinning like a Cheshire cat when I looked at her.

"What?" I asked.

"Nothing. Just glad I lost a bet to my wife."

It took me a moment to realize she'd seen my exchange with James and came to the right conclusion. I looked at James and smiled. He smiled back at me.

No, I didn't care if my family was about to find out about James and I. If recent events were anything to go by, then I wanted to make the most of my life, and that included letting my family in, showing them who I was and who I wanted to be with.

JAMES

As soon as we arrived at the police station, I excused myself to the bathroom. If Connor noticed my strange behavior, he didn't say anything, but I was thankful he didn't follow me.

I checked all the cubicles to make sure I really was on my own before I banged my fist against the tiled wall and kicked the trash can to the other side of the room, leaving a trail of tissue before coming to a stop by the door.

How could have I let this happen? What a fucking great professional I was, being saved by the person I was meant to be keeping safe. How fucking incompetent.

Images of Connor lying dead on his kitchen floor, of his body being found burned beyond recognition ran through my mind. I couldn't see anything in front of me but his pale skin, his bright green eyes dull, lifeless. My hand throbbed as I hit the wall again and then looked up at the mirror.

"What a fucking hero you are, Captain Bennett."

I shook my head at my reflection and then noticed something. A small reddish bruise on the side of my neck. My eyes filled with tears as I remembered the exact moment I'd felt Connor bite my skin and suck on it during our shared shower.

There was only one thing I could do to fix this. I took my phone out and dialed.

"Hello, this is the phone of His Royal Nakedness. This is Charlie speaking. How may I be of assistance?"

Despite my inner turmoil, I couldn't stop a laugh as I heard Kris in the background shouting "Charlie!" and then rustling noises...moans?...and then finally the voice I was hoping to hear.

"Who is this?" Kris asked a little out of breath.

"It's only me. Having a good time?" I teased.

"Um...yeah..." He chuckled. "What's up?"

"I know I can make this decision without asking, but I respect you too much, so I'm just going to say it. I'm going back to Lydovia, so I need Ryan to get back here."

"What happened?"

"I screwed up, let my guard down, and Connor nearly...never-mind. I think it's best if I'm not here because I'm a risk—"

"Let me stop you there," Kris said, interrupting me. "Let's pretend for a second I actually believe the bullshit you're about to spout at me. How does Connor feel about you leaving?"

"He doesn't know," I confessed.

"So, something happens, and after spending a week looking out for him and nursing him back to health, when the going gets tough, you decide to run."

"No, that's not..." I groaned. Didn't he get it?

"Would you stay with Charlie knowing you couldn't be focused enough to keep him safe?" I asked, trying to keep my voice steady but failing miserably.

Kris laughed.

What the hell?

"James, sometimes you can try to do what's best for someone or they take the decision out of your hands by doing what's right in the first place."

I let out a long, frustrated breath and leaned against the back wall, pressing the back of my head against the cold tiles. I knew what he meant. A year ago Charlie had done just that for Kris. By coming forward with their relationship, he put himself in the firing line of the press. Even if Kris had wanted to protect Charlie, I knew Charlie well enough by now to know he would always do the right thing.

The door of the bathroom slammed open, and suddenly, I was faced with a furious-looking Connor.

"Kris, let me call you back," I said before I disconnected the call. "What—"

I didn't have a chance to ask him what was wrong before he crossed the small area and slammed his lips onto mine with such force it took my breath away. My phone dropped on the floor with a crack as I cradled Connor's head with my hands.

He pushed me into the wall with the force of his body, and his hands sought mine, gripping my wrists and holding them above my head. I lost all sense of what was wrong or right, or even what the fuck my name was and where I came from, because for whatever reason, Connor had decided to take control, and my body was so ready for it.

I wouldn't even say no if he decided to pull my trousers down and fuck me right here against the sink with very little prep. The thought that he might not even carry a condom with him got me even harder than I already was from his assault on my mouth.

Connor was only a tad shorter than me, and even though he wasn't as big, he was by no means a small man. I never thought I had a type before, but Connor was very much my type. One encounter, one blowjob, and he already owned me. *Fuck.*

I was getting ready to blow in my pants when Connor stopped kissing me. He leaned his forehead against mine as we both caught our breath. He was still holding my hands above my head.

"Please tell me you liked that," he said panting.

"Liked that? Baby, you nearly blew my head off." I chuckled.

"Then why do you want to leave me?"

He pulled his head back, and I looked into his beautiful green eyes that were shiny with unshed tears.

I moved my arms, and he released my wrists so I cradled his face between my hands.

"I'm sorry. I don't really want to leave you, but I'm so fucking scared, Connor. What if I'm putting you at risk because I'm distracted? You saved me from that fire today. I should have been the one who made sure you got out of there safely."

He shook his head. "Don't you see? You did save me. You put yourself in the line of fire for me. Look," he said, stepping back and pointing at his body. "I'm not hurt. I don't even have a scratch on me. Well, maybe a bruised knee since you did push me pretty hard across the room." He smiled.

"How did you know I was considering leaving?" I asked, and he smiled before we both said at the same time.

"Charlie."

"James, in case you haven't noticed, I'm not exactly a damsel in distress," he said. "Let's go out there and figure out who's out to get me and why because there are more important things I want to get to."

Connor stepped forward again, pressing his body against mine and kissing me, his sweet tongue dancing around mine with so much confidence.

"What things?" I said, catching my breath and running my fingers over his freckles.

"Things such as my sister already knowing there's something between us. Things such as wanting to spend more time with you naked. Yeah, especially that second one."

"Fuck, you're going to kill me, Con."

Why was I still surprised at how easily he was accepting his attraction to another man? Even as a kid, Connor had always been the most self-assured and adventurous person I knew.

He pulled me by my hand to lead me out of the bathroom. I released him to pick my phone up from the floor, and when I walked out, I bumped right into his back.

Mrs. Williams came around Connor and put her arms

around my waist. She was so tiny her head only came up to my chest.

"Oh my dear, I'm so glad you're okay. You're okay, right?" she asked, patting my chest and turning me around. I saw Connor smile from the corner of my eye, which made my heart skip at least ten beats.

Once Connor's mom was satisfied that we were all okay, she herded us to Scott's office where the rest of the family was congregated.

We leaned against the door frame side by side since there was not a spare inch of Scott's office that wasn't occupied by a Williams.

"Thank you all for coming so quickly," Scott said. "I know this is highly unusual, but considering the severity of the attack at Connor's house and your relationship with the Lydovian royal family, we need to take precautions."

"Who is doing this to my boy?" Connor's mom asked.

"We have a suspect," Scott said. "James, the kid your colleague identified hasn't turned up for his shift at work today. I spoke to my friend at the gym, and he's going to call me if Brad comes back. At the moment, he's our only suspect, although we don't know what his motive would be."

"Scott, what do you advise as the next steps?" I asked.

He looked around the room, pausing on Hannah and then coming back to me. "We don't know what this guy is capable of, or even if he's on his own. Unfortunately, I don't have the resources to support twenty-four-hour security for everyone."

I raised my hand. "How would everyone feel about visiting Charlie in Lydovia?"

CONNOR

I looked around the room at my family who were taking everything in stride as if house break-ins, threats to life, and fires caused by hand grenades were something they dealt with on a daily basis.

Not that they weren't worried. Aunt Gina was uncharacteristically silent and holding Uncle John's hand, Hannah and Ellie looked at each other as if they were communicating their worries telepathically, and my mom was wringing her hands on her lap and looking down.

"How about Connor?" my dad asked.

"I suspect Scott will need Connor relatively close by to help with the investigation," James said. "I have a place in Windsor. It's safe, and Connor will be secure and have everything he needs there."

"Windsor, England?" Ellie screeched. "Can we come too?"

James tensed a little next to me, but he smiled and said, "No, Windsor, Connecticut."

Ellie deflated, but then my sister reassured her they could visit the real Windsor once this was all over before they flew back from Lydovia.

Suddenly, the whole family started a discussion over which

parts of England they had to visit, with Ellie shouting out all the locations from her favorite romance novels, and Gina talking about going to the theatre in the West End in London.

I turned to James who looked a little lost all of a sudden and whispered, "Hey, are you okay?"

"Yeah," he breathed out.

With all arrangements complete and Ryan on his way in Kris's plane, everyone agreed it would be safer to spend the night together at my parents', despite the shortage of rooms. No one questioned why James slept in my room rather than the sofa in the den.

It wasn't until we were in the car driving to James's house the following morning that I started thinking about all the questions I had, and why all of a sudden it seemed important to get the answers. I looked behind me to the back seat where Bubbles was safely stored in her travel box.

So far, James hadn't told me much about himself or his life after he left Chester Falls, which had left me to fill in the blanks with all kinds of options.

In the last week, we'd spent so much time together talking, watching movies, or playing with Bubbles, but at no point did he mention anything from his personal life apart from sharing stories of his time at college with Kris and then training to serve our country.

I'd wanted to bring up the subjects of his mom and where she had taken them, and why he had never tried to get in touch after he left.

The further away we drove from Chester Falls, the more the landscape around us changed from suburban to countryside, especially once we left the highway. It was a drive I'd done a few times before when I'd visited Charlie in Boston, but I'd never come this way.

Less than an hour later, we pulled up in front of a large iron gate. It looked old like the gates of those haunted houses in movies.

"Are you bringing me here to kill me?" I joked, but James didn't seem to have heard me.

He stepped out of the car to open the gate. It looked heavy and hard to move, so I got out to help him. That was when I noticed the plaque on the wall that said *Lexington Hall*, and a driveway that was so long I couldn't see where it ended.

"Stay there," James said once we opened the gate. He got back in the car and drove it through the gate, parking it just inside and then going back to close the gate behind us. "Come on, let's go for a walk."

James held my hand, and we walked on a small path by the wall surrounding the property until we reached a small stream.

"Who are you?" I asked, unable to keep my questions to myself any longer.

"I'm... Ugh... I'm just James Bennett. Despite anything I might tell you, or anything that you hear or see when we get up to the house, I need you to promise me, Connor." His voice cracked a little.

I put my arms around him and gave him a kiss. "What do you want me to promise, Jamie?"

He smiled at my use of his childhood nickname and kissed me back some more.

"I need you to promise that to you, I'm just James, the same kid you used to hang out with."

I ran my hands up and down his muscled arms, feeling them flexing under my touch.

"Well," I said, "with some improvements." That adorable dimple made an appearance on his cheek, and my heart felt five times bigger. "Nothing you tell me now will change what I already know about you, James."

He took a deep breath and held both my hands. I prepared myself to hear something big, something that had somehow changed my friend, now lover, into what he was today.

"My mom never told me much about my dad. I remember asking her once why she never had a boyfriend, and she shushed me and said she only loved one man in her life, my dad. I think that was the first time I remember her mentioning him at all."

"How old were you?" I asked.

"Eleven, I think. It was just before I moved schools but she never talked about it for another four years. Anyway, I didn't understand why we had to move from Chester Falls until I arrived here. It was late at night, and it was dark. I was taken by this nice lady who brought me to a room and said it was going to be my room from then on." James put his arm around my waist and started walking slowly down the path.

"I didn't see my mom until the next morning when she introduced me to my dad."

His bitter laugh told me it wasn't a pleasant meeting.

"He looked so serious and important that I didn't know how to greet him. He had an accent too. He told me he was Lord George Herbert-Lexington, Earl of Berkshire, and I was to call him Sir. I didn't see him or my mother for weeks after that."

James's grip on my waist was so tight I had to stop him and put my hands around him for a hug.

"Do you want to tell me more? Or do you want to stop?"

I felt his nod even as he had his face buried between my neck and shoulder.

"Mary was great. She and Rupert made me feel really welcome, but I didn't feel at home, and I didn't understand what was happening. No one told me anything. One evening, I stormed into the dining room where my mom and George were having dinner and demanded to know what was going on or I'd go back to Chester Falls.

George didn't even take any notice of me. My mom took me to my room and told me we were going to move to England. She'd worked for George before I was born. They had an affair and she got pregnant. He didn't want anyone to find out, especially his wife, so my mom agreed to move away. She kept working for him all those years, and he never wanted to even meet me. It was like I didn't exist."

"Oh, James." My own voice cracked as I felt for the teenager who'd been lied to all his life and then taken from his world into a new one he didn't understand, only to feel rejected by the one man who should have looked after him.

"He loved my mom so much. I saw it in his eyes," he said, and I heard what he didn't say. That his father's love hadn't extended to him.

"I hated living in England. Not the country so much because it was beautiful there, apart from the weather. But I was told I had to behave in certain ways, and I was sent to a private school full of these rich kids who teased me because of my accent. All I wanted was to come home and find you again. I knew that if I came to Chester Falls, I'd be home again."

"Oh, there you are. Did you think you'd sneak in on me, yer little devil?"

The tiny woman crossed the stream, which fortunately was only ankle deep and she was wearing rubber boots, and put her arms around James. She fussed over him, and I laughed remembering how my mom had done exactly the same only yesterday.

"For a gay man, you have a way with the ladies," I joked.

James was beaming and hugging the woman back.

"And you must be Connor," she said before wrapping her arms around me too. "God, Jesus, and Mary, I once met a lad called Connor from County Cork. So skinny he'd blow over on a windy day. I'm Mary, by the way."

My eyes met James, and I knew that despite everything, Mary had looked after him as he grew up into the man I knew today.

"Come on, boys. Let's get home. I have a lamb casserole with dumplings bubbling away in the pot for lunch."

"You lead the way, Mary." James said as he grabbed my hand and we walked together back to the car.

JAMES

Only Mary had the ability to make me feel at home in the one place that once felt like a prison. I'd never asked Mary why she and Rupert had never had kids even though she was the most maternal person I knew, as was evidenced by how she fussed over Connor and Bubbles as soon as we managed to drive up to the house and get settled.

"This place is like something out of a British movie," Connor said, admiring the manicured gardens from the window of my bedroom.

I wrapped my arms around his waist and kissed the back of his neck, loving how he melted into me.

"Do you want a tour?" I asked.

He turned around and kissed me, his tongue seeking entrance into my mouth immediately as his hands went around my back, massaging the muscles that had only started relaxing once we were safe inside the property.

For once, I was glad to have this place, and since no one knew about it, I was confident Connor would be safe until Scott found out more about the attack.

"Fuck, Con," I gasped as he peppered my jaw and neck with

kisses until he reached that one spot he'd sucked on before. God, had that only been yesterday morning?

"I think I'm happy where I am. We can tour later," he said.

I hissed as his strong hands brushed over my erection and then worked the button and zip of my slacks open. He pushed me backward until I hit the ottoman at the foot of the bed with the backs of my knees, hinting at me to sit down.

"I would love a tour," he said, kneeling down at my feet.

His eyes were so dark with lust it was like I was lost in a dark forest. One that I'd happily get lost in.

"This wasn't the kind of tour I was talking about, but by all means, feel free to explore."

I bent down and kissed him before I leaned back to give him some space. He indicated for me to lift up a little so he could pull my pants down.

He surprised me once again when he pulled both pants and boxer shorts down together, but only to my thighs. Being fully dressed with only my cock exposed turned me on more than I ever thought. How was this man surprising me every step of the way?

"Taking the shortcut, are we?" I teased.

"Uh-huh," he said before taking me in his mouth.

Yesterday, when we'd taken our shower together, I'd let him explore my cock. He hadn't gone down on me, but he'd played and teased until I'd come in his hand. I wanted to take things slow with Connor because all of the stuff we were doing were firsts for him, and I wanted to make them as special as he deserved them to be.

I didn't want to risk losing him by taking things too far or too fast, not that he seemed as worried as me because the way he was sucking on my cock showed how little issue he had with being with a guy.

"Fuck, fuck...ahh," I moaned. "Where did you learn that?"

He eased off my cock, replacing his mouth with his hand and applying additional pressure around my shaft. I leaned back on the bed praying I wouldn't die from this because I was as eager to chase my orgasm as I was to reciprocate.

"I know what I like, baby," he said.

"You seem to know what I like too," I laughed but then moaned again when I felt the heat of his mouth on me once more.

I looked down, and the sight of his head bobbing up and down on my cock was almost too much.

"I'm so close, Con, please don't stop."

He wrapped one hand around my shaft, twisting it as he motioned up and down. With the increased pressure and his tongue teasing my frenulum, I was hopeless to stop my orgasm.

I tried to warn him, but when I touched his head, he sucked me deeper until I came into the back of his throat. He didn't stop his attention to my cock until I was completely spent.

"Jesus, I think I'm dead," I exhaled.

"I'll take that as a compliment," Connor said, crawling over on top of me to seal his mouth over mine in a searing kiss. "How about that tour? The PG-rated one, of course."

"Give me a minute. I may need CPR," I joked.

We kissed lazily, but every time I tried to get closer to Connor's still hard cock, he pushed my hand away.

"I'm saving that for later," he said.

"Then let's get out of the room because I'm not holding myself responsible for keeping my hands off you if we stay here."

Showing Connor the house was like seeing it all over again, but with a new pair of eyes. When I was fifteen, all I saw was old, creepy paintings that looked like they followed you around the rooms, ratty carpets, weird wall hangings, and statues everywhere. It was like stepping into a different world.

"Do you think these guys are related to you?" Connor asked, looking at the various paintings in one of the rooms.

"I don't know, maybe?"

"Okay, your dad was a dick, but wow, look at all this history. Are you related to the queen of England?" he asked.

I laughed. Truth was, I didn't know and wasn't interested in finding out, but going from room to room and answering all of Connor's ridiculous questions made me think about my ancestry for the first time. Not in the way that I thought it had any importance, but just the thought that I'd come from somewhere, even if I hadn't exactly been welcomed back.

"Come on, let me show you the gardens before Mary calls us for food. You don't want to be late when she calls you, or you get fewer dumplings."

"Let's go then, what are we waiting for?" he said as he ran out through the double doors leading to the back.

It had been months since I'd visited, and even longer since I'd ventured into my favorite part of the property. In those first weeks after I'd arrived, the house felt stifling, so the gardens had been my escape.

Unlike the driveway, which was too bare, the gardens were full of trees, manicured lawns, flower beds, and my favorite feature, a pond that attracted birds and ducks and was full of fish.

"This reminds me of that river path from the Old Mill into town," Connor said.

"I know. This was my favorite place when I first came here. It reminded me of home, and school, and you."

"Hey, Master James," Rupert's voice called out from the distance. I waved as I saw my favorite mutt running toward me at a speed. I braced myself for the super excited greeting I always got from Donnie every time I came home.

"Hey, boy, how's life?" As expected, I still ended up on the ground with an excited dog licking me and a too-long tail wagging everywhere.

"Ease up, Donnie, he's not going anywhere," Rupert said, and the dog, as if understanding what his owner meant, got off me to introduce himself to Connor in a similar excited fashion.

"Nice to see you, Rupert. The gardens look amazing," I said, giving the old man a hug. "The person under Donnie is my... um... Connor."

Connor stood up from the ground to shake Rupert's hand as Donnie, a black and white border collie and Jack Russell mix, circled happily around us before he settled on top of my feet.

"We had a good spring this year, Master. You know a lot of it looks after itself, all I do is give it a little helping hand."

I knew he was downplaying his role in the upkeep of the grounds and how much work it really required.

"Rupert, do you need help? Maybe we should hire someone to help you."

"Tell you what, Master James. You fill this big house with a family, and then you'll have a reason to hire someone. For now, I'm happy pottering around and doing what I can."

My heart broke a little for Rupert. I knew how much he loved the house and working outdoors, but I'd never seen the house as my home.

Rupert put his hand on my shoulder and squeezed in understanding, but then he looked at Connor and winked. "Maybe you could help us change his mind."

Mary calling us from the house put a stop to the conversation, but I could tell from how Connor looked at me that we would be revising this topic.

"Come on, last one in has to forfeit a dumpling," I said as I started a run toward the house.

I was nearly there when Connor jumped on my back with the inevitable result that we both fell face-first on the grass. He wrestled me to get back up and get the advantage, but I pulled him back down to me planting a kiss on his lips that left us both stupid and forgetting about dinner until Mary coughed from the door.

"I think we've just been caught," Connor said into my mouth.

"Shhhhh. If we don't move, she won't see us," I said before I tickled him, which caused him to jump away from me.

We laughed all the way to Mary who made the sweetest attempt at a stern face.

CONNOR

I loved Mary, there were no two ways about it. The woman was a hurricane, and she reminded me so much of my mom that I was pretty sure the two women would get on like a house on fire if they ever met. I would almost feel for Rupert and my dad if I thought it wouldn't be so much fun to watch them.

What the hell? Why was I thinking about Mary and my mom meeting or Rupert and my dad becoming friends?

"Mary, how do you feel about marrying me?" I said, leaning back on my chair and patting my stomach. "That was the best stew I've ever had, and don't you dare tell my mother."

"Not a chance, my boy. The woman signed a paper once upon a time, so she's all mine," Rupert said, leaning over and kissing Mary's cheek.

"No need to fight, my dears. There's plenty of Mary for every-one." She got up from the table, taking her dishes to the sink.

"Oh, no you don't, Mary. James and I are on washing up duty. You go... um...have a rest," I shooed her out of the way but not without giving her a hug.

"You'll do, my dear, you'll do," she said, looking up at me with an all-knowing gaze and then got on her tiptoes to reach up to me.

I bent down a little thinking she wanted to give me a kiss, but she just whispered in my ear, "Look after my boy's heart, will you? He's been hurt enough for a lifetime."

She leaned back on her heels and stared into my eyes. I didn't know what to say. What she was asking felt like such an enormous responsibility. Would I look after James's heart? Absolutely. Could I end up hurting him along the way? I wasn't sure. There was still part of me that was still afraid he might try to run again.

I nodded, my words stuck in my throat. She seemed satisfied with my answer because she grabbed the rest of the dishes from the table and left them by the sink.

"Come on, big boy, we have work to do," I called out to James who was in conversation with Rupert and had thankfully missed my exchange with Mary.

Mary and Rupert disappeared, leaving us with the washing up, a job that took longer than normal because James took up every opportunity he could to steal a kiss or grope my ass. I had a massive disadvantage because my hands were wet from the soapy water, but as soon as his started exploring the skin under my shirt, I threw in the towel and gripped his shirt, wet hands and all, and kissed him with everything I had.

"Can we take this up to the bedroom?" James asked.

"Absolutely."

We were both breathless by the time we finished tidying up the kitchen, but I wanted to check on Bubbles before we went up. Even though Mary had said earlier that she'd been well behaved and hadn't escaped once, I was very nervous that she'd get lost in such a big house and we'd never find her.

Her tank was in one of the small sitting rooms. Rupert had said the room was a sun trap in the morning and Bubbles would love it. When we went in, I half expected her to be gone and for my naked plans to go out the window while we went in search of my errant turtle.

Instead, we found Donnie laying on the floor with his head resting on his front paws, tail wagging side to side as he watched Bubbles swimming happily in the tank.

I crouched down and patted his head. He licked my hand but soon after went back to watching Bubbles. Occasionally, she'd come to the glass as if to tease him and he'd raise his head slightly before laying it back down when she ignored him.

"Well, looks like Bubbles has her own bodyguard," I said, wrapping my arms around James's waist. "It's time for me to spend some time with my own. After all, he owes me an orgasm."

"Oh does he?" James said, kissing the tip of my nose. "That's very unprofessional of him. How can he redeem himself?"

I pretended to think about it for a moment before I said, "He can let me fuck him." I bit my lip waiting for his reply, but he froze still. I panicked. Oh shit. "Or you can fuck me... I mean, I've never... but I don't mind what we do... If that's not your thing, then I—"

James stopped my ramble with a kiss and then pulled me by the hand, running up the stairs and not stopping until we were inside the room with the door locked.

He pushed me against the door, trapping my body with his bigger one.

"Fuck, yes, baby. So much...yes." James kissed me again, biting on my bottom lip and then sucking gently. The effect of that went straight to my cock, and I wondered for a moment if I'd last long enough to get past this moment.

I put my hands on James's chest and pushed him back toward the bed, removing his shirt and undoing his trousers at the same time. He helped with his shoes and socks, and in no time, I had him gloriously naked under me.

"God, you're gorgeous," I said, straddling him and removing my own shirt. He used my momentary distraction to flip us over, and suddenly I was on my back with James removing my shoes, trousers, and underwear all in one go.

"Now we're even," he said as he picked up my left leg, kissing my calf, then the back of my knee and down my thigh. He stopped and picked up the other leg, giving it the same treatment.

My hips rose up from the bed in anticipation of his mouth getting somewhere close to my desperately hard cock. "Please James," I begged.

"Please what, baby?" he kept teasing, kissing me everywhere except where I really wanted his mouth. "I love your pale skin, your freckles, your strong body...can't wait to feel you inside me."

I'd been writhing on the bed, my short, sharp intakes of breath a direct cause of his touch, but when he said he wanted me to be inside him, I stopped breathing altogether.

"Do...do you really want that?" I asked.

He crawled up my body, settling his weight on me, our cocks rubbing deliciously against each other, and wrapped his hand around the back of my neck to keep me in place.

"I want that more than I want my next breath, baby... please?"

I nodded.

He reached out for his bedside table and took out a condom and a small bottle of lube from the top drawer.

"How do you want me?" he asked.

"On your back. I want to see you."

He settled in the middle of the bed and opened his legs to give me some room. I kneeled and sat back on my heels.

My mouth felt dry all of a sudden. James was strong, beautiful, and could probably get anyone he wanted in his bed, but here he was, opening himself to me. I swallowed and looked into his eyes.

His brows were drawn together, and I saw the worry in his eyes.

Doubt suddenly filled my every pore. "What if I don't do it right?" I said in such a low voice I wasn't sure he'd heard me.

James sat up and took my hand, placing it on his cock. I loved the contrast of the soft skin over the warm hardness.

"Do you feel this, Connor? This is for you, only you. I don't sleep around, and I don't get this hard for just anyone. Do you hear me?"

I nodded, incapable of voicing all the feelings swirling inside my chest.

He took the condom from my hands, ripped the foil, and rolled it down my length. Then he picked up the bottle and was about to squirt some of the lube on his fingers when I snapped the bottle from his hands.

My fingers trembled as I squirted a little bit of lube on my fingers and ran them over his hole. It's not that I didn't know what to do, because since I'd discovered my attraction to James, I'd been online doing some research.

Porn was a rabbit hole of things you didn't want to see but couldn't stop watching, but it had also yielded some interesting further research.

James had his eyes closed, but he looked relaxed enough when I tried adding my first finger. The heat and tightness was unlike anything I could have expected. How the fuck would my cock fit in there?

I pulled the finger out and pushed it back in again, the second time curving it slightly in search of the sensitive bundle of nerves I'd read would drive him wild.

As I increased my pace, James opened his eyes, his mouth slightly open and gasping for air.

"Fuck, another one...I need more," he said.

I added another finger, but it seemed I was too slow because he pulled me on top of him and said into my mouth, "Screw that, I need you. I need you inside me right now."

He didn't let go of me, so I added some more lube to my fingers and spread it over my sheathed cock hoping it was enough. I grabbed my dick and tried my best to point it at his entrance.

As soon as the head of my cock was in, I thought my own head was going to explode from the heat, tightness, and sheer pleasure. Sweat was running down my back, and I had to close my eyes because staring into James's was just too much all at the same time.

I knew it would feel good having Connor push his way inside me, but the rest? How could have I guessed?

My body welcomed him as if it had been waiting all its life for us to come together like this. My skin tingled all the way to the tips of my fingers.

Connor looked at me as if he was worried he'd hurt me or go too fast too soon.

He pushed further, sweat running down the side of his temple. I cleared it with my hand, which made him look at me rather than where we were joined together.

"It feels so good, baby," I said, pulling him for a kiss and then moaning when his cock brushed against my prostate.

The change in Connor when he was finally all the way in and let out a choked, almost pained breath was as clear as the green in his eyes.

"James..." He cried.

"It's okay, baby. Take a deep breath. Can you move for me? I need to feel you."

He obeyed and started at first with slow, steady moves, increasing his pace the easier it became to glide in and out of me.

The way my cock was trapped between us caused so much delicious friction, and with Connor brushing past my prostate with each move, it didn't take long for the familiar tingle to rise up my spine.

"Con, I'm close," I warned.

He put his arms under my shoulders and cradled my head, making sure my focus was solely on him. As if it would be anywhere else when my whole world at this moment was just him.

"I'm going to give you what you need, baby. Trust me?" he asked.

"Implicitly."

"Wrap your legs around my waist," he said.

As soon as I did, he pushed further in, going deeper than before. Connor increased his pace until he was relentlessly fucking me, hitting all the right spots. It was almost too much and not enough.

"Open your eyes," he commanded.

At first, I didn't want to look at him because I was too afraid that my feelings would spill out, but at the same time I needed to know what was going through Connor as we chased our release.

What I saw staring back at me through his gaze was what I'd been too afraid to hope for. And that stupid little word, *hope*, made my heart soar so high that when my orgasm finally came, I wondered if I was actually having an out of body experience.

Connor's orgasm came shortly after, his jerky movements causing my own orgasm to prolong.

We didn't speak for a while, the only sound in the room coming from our joint breaths and small kisses as we recovered.

His arms were still tight around me as if he didn't want me to move. Not that I'd ever want to, and besides, my brain was still in too much of a mushy state to do or say anything other than hold on.

When Connor finally moved, I felt the loss instantly. If there was a possibility that I could keep Connor glued to me for the rest of my life, I'd take it in a heartbeat.

"Hmm, I could get used to this," I said as I woke up the next morning with Connor naked and half on top of me.

"Do you hear me arguing?" he said before coming up from where his head was resting on my chest and giving me a morning kiss.

I wanted to drag it out and take it further, but Connor, the tease he was, got up and pulled my hand toward the shower with a look that said *washing only allowed*. Luckily, I had my own ways of persuasion and ended up plastered against the wall of the shower as Connor took me from behind.

When we finally made it downstairs, Mary had left us a packed breakfast with a note.

I'd say don't eat it all but I know you all too well, James. Love, Mary.

"Let's take this outside to the pond," I suggested.

"Oh my god. What's that smell?"

I smiled and opened the box, raising it up to his nose. Connor inhaled the scent of the filled, flaky pastry, and his stomach rumbled at the same time as he rolled his eyes back.

"Welcome to the world of Mary's sausage rolls," I said. "Come on, let's get outside."

As soon as we found a spot by the pond under a tree, I felt like I'd swallowed a happy pill. The smell of the freshly cut grass, the birds chirping in the background, and Connor sitting next to me with his knee bumping into mine. This was perfection.

I filled our cups with the coffee Mary had brewed into a thermos for us and nearly burned myself when Connor tried a sausage roll and moaned his appreciation.

"I'm going to take offense, you know?" I said.

"You should. These are better than sex." He took another one, and I had to steal the box from him or I'd be missing out on breakfast.

"If you think these are better than sex, then we've been doing it wrong, baby," I said putting a roll in my mouth and wondering what Mary had done to her recipe because these were better than I remembered. When I moaned, too, Connor gave me a dirty look. Maybe we should have taken breakfast up to the room rather than outside where we could be seen.

"So, tell me how you've come to own this place," Connor asked.

I debated telling him, but he was here now, and apart from the fact Mary couldn't keep her mouth shut, it just felt good to share this stuff with Connor.

"I never understood why, but George left it to me in his will," I said.

"Why? You were his son, after all."

"I have a half brother and sister. We don't talk much. After George died, they thought they'd get the house." I finished my coffee and put the cup down on the blanket. "They've been wanting to buy the house from me for years. At first, I said no because I felt that my mom deserved to have somewhere nice to live, but then she was gone too."

I never thought too much about my mom and how she'd died of a broken heart, too sad to carry on living after the only man she loved all her life had died from a short illness. Even I hadn't been reason enough for her to carry on.

"Hey," Connor said, cleaning the tears running down my face and then placing a soft kiss on my lips.

"She wasn't happy enough with me. I wasn't enough for her to keep going. Even when I thought it was just me and her, I had been wrong because she'd got on a bus every day and traveled almost an hour each way so she could continue working for him."

I'd gone into the military straight after my mom's death in a show of defiance toward my father, who'd despised everything American even though he'd been happy enough living in the country. It had also been a good excuse to keep away from my siblings and their increased pressure to sell the house.

"How about now? How do you feel about the house?"

I looked around us. I'd never called this place my home, but Mary and Rupert had been my surrogate parents since I'd turned up as a gangly, skinny, and angry teenager. They'd become my home.

"I don't know. Part of me wants to sell the house. God knows my brother and sister have wanted it for years. They've only stopped short of contesting the will because Mary put the fear of god in them."

"But...?"

I took a deep breath and pulled his hands up to my mouth, kissing his palm. He cradled my face caressing my short scruff.

"But this is Mary and Rupert's home too. My personal history with this place isn't great, but I'm starting to think it doesn't have to be that way. Having you here with me is making me see the house differently."

Connor tilted his head sideways and scrunched up his eyes, and I smiled at his adorable thinking face.

"Have you thought about turning it into a hotel, or a place you can host events in, like weddings or celebrations?"

I had never thought of this place being anything more than just a home, and because I struggled to see it as a home for myself, I guess I hadn't seen any other possibilities.

"I already have a job," I said. "And I wouldn't have a clue where to start. I'm not a businessman."

Connor got up and held his hand for me.

"Come on, let's go play with Bubbles. I bet she misses you." He winked. "You don't have to figure anything out right now."

As soon as I was on my feet, I put my arms around Connor's waist and lifted him up. He wrapped his legs around my waist, but he was too heavy, so we ended up back on the ground laughing our butts off.

"You're quite amazing. You know that, Connor Williams?"

"I've been told once or twice. Mostly it's because of the size of my—"

I silenced him with a kiss and felt his laugh against my lips. He wasn't entirely wrong in his statement.

My perfect day came to a halt when we approached the back door to the kitchen and I heard the voices of my half-siblings.

CONNOR

We were joking and laughing on the way back to the house when James stopped short of the back door to the kitchen.

I heard voices inside, but the only one I recognized was Mary's Irish accent.

"What's the matter?" I asked.

James turned around, placed our breakfast setup on the ground, and started walking back to where we'd come from.

"James, wait. What's up? Who's in there?" I asked, catching up with him just as he followed the path by the pond toward an area that was more built up with trees. He was walking so fast I thought he might break into a run.

"My brother and sister," he said, his fists clenched on either side of him. "Why did they have to fucking come here today?"

It was hard to read him because he sounded angry, but I could tell there was something else too. I went around him to make him stop.

"Talk to me, James."

He stared at me before his lips came down on mine. He ran his fingers through my hair, and the feeling of his blunt nails on my scalp followed by a gentle pull of my hair as he deepened the kiss got me instantly hard.

"Is distracting your opponent something you learned in the military?" I asked, pulling back from the kiss and walking backward.

He chuckled. "This particular distracting tactic has never been tested, but I can see it works. I'll have to make a note and add it to my list of skills," he said, looking down at my jeans where my erection was noticeable.

I crossed my arms and stopped. He kept coming forward until we were nose to nose.

"What do you want me to do?" he asked.

"I want you to go back there and find out what they want. Then send them on their way so we can work your tension off in bed."

His intense gaze softened, and he smiled wide enough that my favorite dimple in the world came out on display. I put my arms around his shoulder and kissed his cheek.

"That's my man," I said with a wink.

He ran his hands up and down my back, leaving them to rest on my hips.

"Do you promise we get sexy time afterward?"

I did a cross sign over my heart with my left hand followed by a mock boy scout salute.

"You dumb ass, the boy scout salute is made with the right hand," he said.

I pressed my body closer to his and cupped his cock before I innocently said, "I never said I was a boy scout."

He shook his head and gave me a kiss before walking back.

"Go get 'em tiger," I shouted at him, and he turned back just before going through the door to stick his tongue out and give me the bird.

I picked up the remains of our breakfast and walked through the kitchen door shortly after, expecting to see Mary. She wasn't there, so I cleared up and decided to see how Bubbles was doing.

Just like yesterday, I'd found Donnie laying by the tank totally fixated on Bubbles. His head was perched on the edge of the tank with Bubbles sunning herself on one of the rocks and staring back at him.

"Hey boy, are you looking after my baby girl?" I said sitting cross-legged on the floor and running my hand down Donnie's shiny brown coat. "I'll have you know she doesn't give her heart up for just anyone, so you be good to her, okay?"

He whimpered and then licked my hand before going back to the subject of his affection. His tail wagged from side to side landing with little thuds on the carpeted floor.

"Is it just her heart you're talking about, me dear?" Mary said, coming in the room holding a tray in her hands. "Come have a coffee with me. I have biscuits too."

"Biscuits?" I asked, wondering why we'd be having biscuits with coffee.

"Oh, I can never get used to your American words even after all these years. I mean cookies."

"In that case, I'm so here for it," I said, getting up off the floor and sitting on one of the couches.

She poured the coffee in a fancy cup and then added milk and sugar to hers. I held my hand to leave mine black and tried one of her shortbreads.

"These are delicious, Mary."

"It's me Nana's recipe, she taught me how to make them when I was only a young lass back in Ireland, but we don't want to talk about that. We want to talk about matters of the heart."

I laughed and sat back waiting for whatever wise words Mary had for me.

"Are you in love with my boy?" she asked.

"Jesus, Mary, you don't pull any punches, do you?"

She laughed out loud. "Son, I've lived through difficult times, and I came through each and every one of them. I'm also too old to waste time with niceties."

"Fair enough," I said, and she gestured for me to continue. "I don't know, Mary. We've only just reconnected after I spent half my life hating him for disappearing on me. Add to it a layer of my newly found attraction to a man, and I'm not sure if I can tell where's up and where's down."

She smiled and nodded her understanding.

I looked out toward the flowery garden. How did I feel about James? There was no doubt that my feelings for him went beyond attraction.

When I'd seen him a year ago I wanted to hate him, mostly for appearing out of nowhere at a time when I was already struggling with so much. But even then, part of me wanted to hug him and not let go. That had been the confused teenager in me that hadn't expected his best friend to kiss him, and expected even less to like it.

For a whole year, I'd waited to see him come back with Kris and Charlie, but he never did. Even now I'd been too afraid to ask him why.

I nearly dropped my empty coffee cup when Mary put her hand on my arm.

"Don't forget he's only human. He may hurt you too. Just remember, it won't be intentional. Deep down he's still that scared boy that was uprooted from his home by two people who were so blindly in love they forgot about the most important person in their lives."

She gave me a hug and left me to my thoughts.

Bubbles and Donnie were still in their staring match. I wasn't sure what it meant that my turtle hadn't tried to escape once since we'd arrived. Was she finally at home?

I wished I could promise her that much, but I didn't know what the future held for us two. All I knew was that I had a burned down house—something I didn't even want to think about, and I was probably developing deep feelings for someone who could leave at any moment.

Maybe a walk would help me clear my head. After all, there

wasn't much I could do about any of it. Scott hadn't got in touch with any further information about the case, and James was currently in a heated discussion, if the raised voices coming from one of the rooms was anything to go by.

I walked around the property toward the driveway, intending on going back to the front gate to find the little stream we'd walked to yesterday.

Rupert called me when I was a third of the way down. I waved and walked through the grass until I reached him. He was kneeling down on the ground, and it looked like he was planting some seedlings. I smiled to myself remembering the last time I'd seen Olly.

"Rupert, I have a little bag with lilac seeds. Would you like to plant them here?" I asked.

He stood up and looked at me. Really looked at me. For some reason, I felt really exposed.

"Lilacs take a long time to grow and flower. I hope you're planning on sticking around to see them grow. It would be a shame to leave them behind, don't you think?"

"Um...I...I'll think about it, Rupert."

He nodded, and I left him with his flowers. When I got back to the driveway, I looked toward the house and realized it was the first time I was taking it in.

If Ellie were here, she would be mentioning something about British movies and Regency romance. Grand was the only word I could use to describe the house, and I could only imagine how James felt when he saw it for the first time.

An image of cars parked in front of the house, children and a couple of dogs running around came to mind, and I had to put my hand on my chest when it felt like my heart skipped a beat.

I nearly fell down on my knees when I realized I'd fallen in love with James. Or, what was even more likely was that I'd been in love with him from the moment I asked him if I could go to the library with him when we were only twelve.

I looked up to the house and saw him behind a window staring into the distance.

How would I move on when he eventually left me again after I'd just found him?

JAMES

After spending the majority of the day locked in a room with my step-siblings, all I wanted was to find Connor and lose myself in him.

It had been a year since I'd had to do this dance with Eliza and Archie. Somehow, even then, they'd known I was home within days of my arriving. I had a suspicion Mary was behind this forced meeting.

She'd always encouraged us to get along. "The blood of the covenant is thicker than the water of the womb. Remember, you have more that keeps you together than what keeps you apart." She'd say every time we all fought.

Being an only child, I'd always wanted siblings, so when we moved to England and I met Eliza and Archie, I thought I'd finally have someone my own age to hang out with.

They, on the other hand, had made it clear from the beginning that neither me nor my mom belonged there. They refused to accept that I was George's son, but what hurt the most was that my mom had helped raise them both since they were born.

I was still holding on to the bitter pill from the past, knowing she'd spent day after day with them, taking them to school, making sure they had everything they needed, while I'd been mostly on my own, doing everything I could to help her when she came home tired from work.

As adults, my mom and George had done everything wrong, but my mom didn't deserve to be treated as she was by the two children she'd given more to than her own.

It was this unhealthy resentment that ate me up inside and made me want to sell the house to anyone that wasn't Eliza and Archie. I hated them enough to do it, but I also loved Mary and Rupert enough to not do it, and that was the permanent stand-off of my life.

"Where is he, Mary?" I asked, stopping by the kitchen after going around the entire house and failing to find Connor.

"Oh yes, Mary, thank you for the sandwiches you so lovingly prepared for our dinner, Mary," she said, pretending to be upset.

"Thank you for the sandwiches, Mary. They were delicious as always," I said, giving her a big kiss on the cheek. "Now, tell me where I can find my man before I go insane."

She put both her hands on my face and said, "He's outside. He said he was going for a walk by the pond."

I kissed her forehead and ran outside. It was already dark, but with a full moon and the solar lights Rupert had installed all over the grounds, I found Connor's silhouette by the pond in no time.

He squealed when I wrapped my hands around him from behind and nuzzled his neck. It was a particularly sensitive and ticklish spot for him, so I carried on kissing it until he was crying for mercy.

"God, I missed you," I said, turning him around and kissing him like I hadn't seen him in weeks. He melted against me, and I felt his hands twist into the fabric of the back of my shirt. I loved how he wasn't afraid to show me how desperate he was for my touch.

"Good meeting?" he asked.

"It never is, but I don't want to talk about it. I want to spend time with you." I kissed his mouth and then his jaw, paying attention to every square inch of skin I could tease. "And now, I want to get naked. Like, very naked."

"Uh-huh," he mumbled while holding the back of my neck to keep me in place as I kept going down, tracing his collarbone, his chest, and moving to pay the same attention to the other side.

"Have you eaten?"

He nodded.

"Thank god. I don't think I can wait a minute longer."

I kissed his lips again and then started walking back to the house, holding on to his hand.

"Wait," he said.

"What's up?"

"Are you sure you're okay?" he asked.

"I started the day very okay, then it was shit, and now I'm counting on erasing the middle part of my day and finishing it the way it started."

He walked past me still hand in hand, pulling me with him toward the house. "I'm on board with that. Very on board."

Unlike all the other mornings since that first one when Connor asked me to stay with him, when I woke up this time, I was on my own. Connor was a total cuddle bear in bed, so even before I was fully conscious, I'd known he wasn't with me.

The bedsheets were cold, too, which was unusual. I got up and got dressed, thinking I'd make the kitchen my first stop. In the last few days, I'd seen him get closer and closer to Mary, so it wouldn't surprise me if he'd gotten up and gone downstairs so he wouldn't disturb my sleep.

We'd been up until very late, wrapped up in each other, making love and laughing.

My phone rang as I was halfway down the stairs, so I ran back to the room to pick it up.

"Hello?"

"Hi James, Scott here. Look, I know there hasn't been any developments for a while, but I just wanted to catch up with Connor and ask him a few questions. It seems Brad is related to an ex-employee from Connor's job. I'm wondering if he can give us a little more information on that employee."

"Sure, Scott. We'll come down to the station later."

I pocketed the phone and ran down the steps to the first floor and straight to the kitchen. It had been years since I'd spent so much time in this house, and I could count using the fingers on one hand how many rooms I'd actually been in. Maybe Connor had something there with his idea to make more of this house.

"Morning, Mary. You're looking beautiful as always," I said, grabbing her by the hand and giving her a twirl before placing a kiss on her cheek.

"You're in a good mood, or did you just smell the cinnamon as you came down the stairs?"

I pretended to be shocked. "You think I'd be so fickle as to pepper you with attention just because I could smell my favorite cinnamon rolls even before I woke up?"

She raised a brow. "They're in that basket there." She pointed, and I beelined for them, putting half of one in my mouth and taking another one out of the basket.

"Greedy boys don't get banana loaf."

"You'd never do that to me," I tried my best to say considering I had a mouth full of cinnamon roll.

"Where did you leave your manners?" she said, placing her hands on her hips.

Before I answered, she put her hand up. "Don't tell me, just go find them."

"Have you seen Connor?" I asked.

"No dear, but Eliza and Archie are in the study."

I groaned. "Why aren't they leaving me this time? We've done the talking and the arguing. Surely I'm good for another year."

"I don't understand why the three of you can't find a way to get along, it's like you're refusing to grow up. Jesus, Mary, and Joseph, if I could I'd give you all a good hiding."

I got out of her reach before she could hit me with her wooden spoon as she often threatened and made my way to the study.

"She's adorable, isn't she?" I heard Eliza say. She was crouching down by Bubbles' tank.

"Hmm," Archie replied noncommittally.

Donnie was on the floor next to the water tank looking like she'd jump at Eliza if she dared to touch Bubbles. Who knew Rupert's dog would develop such strong feelings for my boyfriend's pet?

I gasped at the direction of my thoughts. Unfortunately, I did it out loud giving away my presence.

"James," Eliza said standing up.

"What do you want? Look, I'm tired of this back and forth that leads nowhere," I said.

They looked as defeated as I felt. Did Mary have a point? She seemed to always be right.

I sat on the sofa that faced the double doors and looked out toward the garden. It was a beautiful sight, and now I wondered why I didn't enjoy it more often, and why I wasn't sharing it with someone else.

"Okay, I have a proposal. It's not my idea, but it could be something with potential."

They both looked at me with such hope that I almost felt sorry for how I'd behaved toward them.

"I'm not selling the house. This is Mary and Rupert's house, and maybe one day, it'll be mine too. But it is a big house and there's plenty of space and rooms that aren't currently used. The whole place is in need of some redecorating and renovating. This isn't something I can do on my own, but I'm wondering if you'd like to start a business with me. We invest equal amounts into the renovation of the house, and when it's done, we open part of the house and garden for events such as weddings and celebrations."

When I finished, they were both staring at me with their mouths open.

"So?"

"Yes!" they both said at the same time.

"That's such an excellent idea. God, James, I have an interior design degree I've never put to good use," Eliza said, linking her hands in front of her chest as if she couldn't wait to get started.

Archie just nodded. He was never a big talker.

"Okay, we can iron out the details another time. Now, if you'll excuse me, I need to go find my boyfriend."

I got up, but as soon as I did, Mary came running into the room.

"James, my dear, Connor is gone."

"What do you mean, *gone*?"

My heart sank when the first thought that popped into my head was that he was running again. He'd been a little quiet the last few days, but I thought it had something to do with the investigation and that we hadn't heard from Scott. Maybe there was more to it. Maybe he was having doubts about us.

"Dear?" Mary said to get my attention. "Bubbles is still here."

I looked at the tank. She was right. He would never go anywhere without her, which could only mean one thing.

Fuck.

CONNOR

y hands shook so much on the steering wheel that it was a surprise how I didn't manage to crash the car.

The text message replayed in my mind as if I was still looking at it.

Come to the Falls Bar parking lot. On your own. If you bring anyone, especially your little bodyguard boyfriend, you can say goodbye to your little friend.

I'd woken up early and was staring at James's sleeping face, trying to decide if today was going to be the day that I told him how I felt about him. When my phone dinged with a text message, I almost ignored it, but since I'd needed to use the bathroom, I picked it up on the way.

The phone nearly fell out of my hands and onto the bathroom floor when I read the message.

Attached to the text was a photo of Tom working on his window display at Fabulize.

The instructions had been clear enough, so I picked up James's car and drove off. I tried not to think about how worried he'd be when he found me gone.

I especially tried not to think about the possibility that he'd think I was leaving him. Leaving a message had been too dangerous because I wasn't sure how quickly behind me he'd be, but since I wouldn't leave without Bubbles, I'd hoped he'd know deep in his heart that I wasn't going out of choice.

The parking lot was empty, but as soon as I parked, my phone dinged again, and a message appeared on my screen.

Step out of the car. Leave the phone on the seat. No messing around. I can see you.

I did as I was told. As I looked for the key to turn the car off, I remembered it was James's rental. Would it have a tracking device? I prayed it did. Maybe if James contacted the car rental company, they'd track the car. I left my phone with the screen facing up. If he showed up here and called me, he might see the texts.

"Move slowly," a voice younger than I'd expected spoke. There was something cold pressed against my neck, which I assumed was a gun. I raised my hands, and he took the car keys from me and threw them away into some nearby bushes.

"What do you want from me," I said, trying to keep calm.

"Shh, it's not time to talk yet. Let's go."

He put his hand on my elbow to turn and directed me toward the overgrown path I knew led to the cave.

"Where are we going?" I asked.

"To your little secret hideaway. Although it's not so secret anymore since I know where it is."

His laugh was so cold it was borderline demonic.

"No messin' about. I'm not afraid to use this gun," he said.

I wanted to ask why the games, why not just use the fucking gun, but I needed to buy some time. I needed to get him to talk because the longer I prolonged the inevitable, the better the chance of James coming to the right conclusion.

If only the little devil in the back of my mind didn't keep on telling me James would never come. He'd truly believe I was gone, and by the time he figured it out, it would be too late. A cold shiver ran down my spine at the thought.

When we arrived at the cave, everything there was torn apart. The nice blankets were all shredded to pieces, and the candles had been thrown everywhere. Even the walls had been graffitied.

Tears built in the back of my eyes, but I tried my best to keep them at bay. Until I knew more about this guy, I couldn't show any weakness.

I was about to turn around to face him when something hit the back of my head, and everything went dark.

~

My head hurt, and I struggled to focus when I tried to open my eyes. A punch landed on my jaw, but when I tried to move away, I realized I was tied down.

As my eyes came into focus, I saw the guy come at me, but instead of punching me again, he pulled me by the collar of my shirt to help me into a sitting position.

With my hands tied behind my back, the only thing I could do was grip the stone wall behind me to avoid toppling over since my feet were also tied together.

How many times had I run through all the possible people who might want to harm me? Former co-workers, people I'd been forced to fire by bosses who only looked at the bottom line.

Not in a million years I'd have thought that my attacker, the person who violated my personal space and put my family at risk, was someone I didn't know.

"Who are you?" I asked. The kid couldn't be older than eighteen or nineteen. He was skinny, but he held himself as if he were strong enough to hold his own in a fight.

"Every day for months I heard my mom come home and talk about her boss. Mr. Williams this, Mr. Williams that. It was a good thing my dad isn't around anymore, because for a while, I thought she was having an affair. She talked about you all the fucking time. Saying it was because of you she got a promotion and we were saving so I could make the trip of a lifetime."

He pointed the gun at me as he spoke, as if I could even make a run for it.

How long had I been out? Would James be on his way?

"Where did you want to go on your trip?" I asked, trying to keep my voice even despite how much it made me nervous that his hands were shaking so much.

"Have you ever heard of the Red River Gorge?"

I shook my head.

"It's the best climbing location in the world."

"You wanted to go there?"

"No, I'm telling you this for the fun of it. Of course I wanted to go there," he said, his voice rising and echoing around the cave. "Did you know the Prince was there once? He told me about it when he and your brother came to the gym. He's real nice." His voice lowered a little. "Must be nice to have so much money you can do what you like."

"What's your name?" I asked.

"Brad."

"Do you need money to go to the Red River Gorge, Brad?"

"It's too late now. The team I wanted to go with has already left. They wouldn't hold my space unless I could pay everything up front."

"I'm sorry, Brad."

He paced the cave, looking at me and pointing the gun. My heart was racing so much I was scared he'd hear it and it would set him off.

"You're sorry? *You're* sorry? It's too fucking late for being sorry," he shouted, getting closer to me.

"Is Linda your mom?" Linda, the woman I so reluctantly fired. Was Brad her son?

He nodded.

"She was great, Brad. You have to believe me, I didn't want to fire her, but I didn't have a choice."

He laughed.

"You know who didn't have a choice? Me. All the money I'd

saved up for my trip, do you know what happened to it? I had to use it so my little sister could get the medical treatment she needed because my mom wasn't covered by health insurance. I didn't have a fucking choice!"

"I'm so sorry, Brad, I—"

"Stop it! Stop trying to be my friend and pretend to understand me so I can let you go."

I laid my head back on the wall behind me and took a deep breath.

"What are you going to do, Brad? You have a gun, so you could hurt me or kill me. What would happen then? You'd run away? How would that help your mom or your sister? Why don't you let me help you?"

He looked at me as if he was considering it. My stomach dropped when he shook his head.

"It's too late. My boss keeps calling me, and he's tight with the police detective, so they probably know everything by now."

"How would they know? Brad, why don't we settle this? Nothing bad has to happen. I can claim everything I've lost on insurance, and I can still help you. I'll make sure that everyone knows I don't want to press charges."

He sat down on the rock looking dejected.

"Please, Brad. I know you're in a difficult situation, but if we work together, I can help you. If you carry on with this, then it may be too late. Don't do anything you can't come back from."

"I can't," he whispered, holding his gun up.

The tears I'd been fighting off were finally allowed to run free. I thought of my family and hoped they'd pull through together. It would be painful, but they'd support each other.

James, my Jamie. My heart broke for him because he would never know how much I loved him. If there was one person who deserved to know how much they were loved, it was him.

I closed my eyes tight and pulled up the image of James sleeping so peacefully this morning. Hopefully, that would carry me through to the other side.

JAMES

"Think, James, think. Where would he go and why?" I said out loud even though I knew none of the people present knew the answer.

"What's wrong?" Eliza asked.

I ran through the sequence of events as I paced the room. Revisiting it actually helped me get in the right mindset.

"And you say he took your car?" Archie asked.

"Yeah, the rental car... Wait," I said, stopping in my tracks. The rental company had GPS on all cars. That had been the deciding factor. I'd needed a regular looking car that didn't attract attention toward Charlie and Kris when they were in Chester Falls, and I'd liked that this company seemed to offer all the extras I needed.

I called the company and spoke to a nice lady who said I'd receive an email and a text message with the current coordinates within a few minutes.

Then I called Scott.

"Scott," I said as soon as he picked up the phone. "Connor's missing. I'm waiting on the GPS coordinates for the rental car."

"Are you sure he hasn't just gone out?" he asked.

His question brought me to a halt as I was about to pick up my gun from the dresser in the bedroom.

"What?"

"No one knows where he was, right? How would someone get to him?"

"I don't know, Scott. All I know is that he wouldn't just leave without telling me. What if...what if he got some kind of threat? How easy would it be for someone to get hold of his phone number?"

I was ready to present him with a dozen more scenarios, but fortunately, I didn't need to.

"How long has he been gone?"

"Don't know. When I woke up, he wasn't here, but I thought he was out for a walk. It's possible that he could have left as early as two hours ago."

Oh my god, what if I was too late already? I didn't want to even consider that option, or that I'd just implied I'd known exactly when Connor got up in the morning.

I put Scott on speakerphone while I put on my shoulder holster and made sure my gun was loaded. Then I put a jacket on. The last thing I wanted was to worry Mary if she saw me carrying a gun.

Despite knowing I was in the military, Mary didn't like that there were guns in the house, so whenever I was home, my gun was always tucked away somewhere safe.

"Text me the details of your car, and I'll do a drive around town," Scott said. "As soon as you have the location, send me another message. If he was really drawn out with a threat, then it's likely he's come back this way."

"Thanks, Scott."

I put the phone in my pocket and went looking for Rupert to borrow his car.

"James," Archie called out from the door before throwing me a set of keys. "Take mine. It'll be faster."

I nodded and ran over to his car. There would be a time when

I'd unpack what this all meant for my relationship with my brother and sister, but for now, my mind was solely focused on trying to get to Connor, wherever he was.

The coordinates for the location of the car came thirty minutes later via a text message. I was just coming to Chester Falls thanks to Archie's Aston Martin. Hopefully, he'd forgive me for breaking every speed limit with his car.

My relief came in the form of an actual address onto my phone because I didn't want to have to stop to enter the coordinates in the navigation system.

The Falls Bar parking lot? Why would someone draw Connor there? As far as I knew, the cave was a well-kept secret between Charlie, Kris, and Connor.

If Connor was at the cave against his will, it only meant that whoever was doing this to him had been watching him for a while.

Scott picked up the phone within one ring.

"Location?"

"Falls Bar."

"What would he do there? The bar is closed, which means you can't go down to the river from the back because they keep the gate closed," he said.

"There's a path at the end of the parking lot that leads down to a small cave. I'm nearly there. If you get there after me, the path starts at the opposite end of the lot. You'll see the start of an overgrown path that looks like it leads nowhere. Follow it until you reach a gate with a sign. The cave is only a few yards downhill from there."

"James..."

"Yeah?"

"I know you're trained for these things, but be careful. The wrong move could put Connor's life at risk," he said.

"See you there, Scott."

I switched the phone off as I turned into the parking lot and saw the car immediately. There was no one around, so I went up to the rental and opened the door with my spare key. Connor's phone was on the driver seat. As soon as I held it up, the screen lit up with unread messages.

The set of instructions on the messages were clear, and for once, I was glad my gut feeling had been right. Connor had spent the last few days showing me exactly how he felt about us without using his words. I knew he wouldn't run out of choice because he loved me as much as I loved him.

The overgrown path made my journey down to the cave painfully slow because I didn't want to alert anyone to my presence. I didn't know if Connor was being held by one or more people.

Fortunately for me, there was a small curve close to the cave wall that allowed me to get close to the entrance without being seen.

I could hear voices on the other side, but the echo inside the cave made it difficult to understand anything. I set my phone to record and put it on the ground and drew my gun, then I peeked around the wall to see how many people were on the other side.

"Why did you threaten Tom?"

Hearing Connor, despite the quavering in his voice, was everything I needed, but then I saw him and had to take a deep breath as my stomach retched. He had a big bruise around his left eye and a cut on his lip.

"I had to find a way to get you here. All your family is hiding away like cowards, and even you fucked off somewhere. Did you go on a little holiday somewhere with your bodyguard boyfriend?"

"He's not—"

"Spare me. I saw how you looked at each other the day of the fire."

His voice was cold and detached. I'd heard it so many times before, and it didn't mean good things.

"I swear, he's nothing to me. We used to be friends a long

time ago. I think he had a crush on me or whatever, but I'm not gay, man."

"Don't you lie to me," the guy shouted, and then I heard a thud.

When I looked again, Connor was laying on the floor, a small trickle of blood coming out of his mouth.

"Fuck," the guy shouted. He stepped away from Connor, which placed him in the ideal position for me. It took me a whole two seconds to disarm him and knock him out.

I kicked his gun to the other end of the cave and then looked for something I could use to tie him. I didn't care that he was only a kid no older than twenty. I found the duct tape he'd brought with him to use on Connor and made sure both his arms and legs were tied tight enough.

As soon as I was sure he couldn't do anything else, I ran over to Connor. He was moving, and his moans of pain were the best sound I'd ever heard.

I was untying Connor's hands when Scott turned up.

"You're late for the party," I said without humor.

"Looks like it. Are they both okay?" he asked.

"The dickhead is going to have a headache, but Connor will need an ambulance. He's just recovered from a concussion and was hit pretty badly in the head again."

Scott helped me take Connor back up the path to the parking lot, and we opened the back door to the rental so Connor could sit. I went around the other side and got in, pulling him tightly against my chest.

He looked at me with those beautiful green eyes that I'd remembered so many times in the years we'd been apart and hopefully would get to look into for the rest of our lives.

"Stay with me, baby. Please." I begged, even as I knew he was trying his best to not close his eyes. "If you stay with me, I promise we'll go back home, and I'll let you fuck me in all the rooms in the house like you wanted last night."

Even his laugh sounded tired. "The hallway?"

"What's that, baby?"

"You'll let me fuck you against the wall in the hallway," he slurred.

"Hell no. I couldn't get a hard-on with those creepy paintings staring at us," I said, trying to inject a little humor. As long as he kept focusing on me, he'd be okay.

"We'll redecorate," he said.

"Anything you want, baby."

"James?" he called in a tiny voice.

"Yeah, baby?"

"I love you."

CONNOR

I felt okay...surprisingly okay, but my head hurt like a bitch, and when I tried to open my eyes, it was like I was being stabbed right through my skull.

"James?" I called, placing my hands over my eyes to shield them from the bright light.

My body didn't feel like it had been shot. That's it, I hadn't been. I remembered when I thought the shot was coming, but instead of a bullet, Brad had used the gun to hit me.

I remember the panic when I saw James from the corner of my eye, and how all it would have taken was for Brad to turn around and he could have shot James.

The rest after that was a little fuzzy, but then the last thing I remember before blacking out was telling James I loved him.

Warmth spread through my body. Whatever happened, he now knew I loved him. I knew he'd heard me because he put his hand on my face and placed a kiss on my forehead.

I heard the sound of a curtain closing and the room darkened. That felt immediately better.

"Hey, honey."

"Tom? Where am I?" I removed my hand from my eyes, and thankfully, with the darker lighting, I was able to see his face.

"You're at the hospital. I'd never been here before, but this is the most adorable place ever."

I smiled at his statement. Only Tom would find a small hospital adorable.

"Don't laugh at me. When you're in pain and have to wait your turn for decades at Boston's Saint Elizabeth's, then you'll know how good you have it here. Anyway, how do you feel?"

"Like someone who doesn't particularly like me hit me on the head with a gun."

This time it was his turn to laugh.

"Where's James? What happened?" I asked.

"They caught the guy. How crazy can people get? Jesus and Coco on a stick, I'd have crapped myself," he said.

"Tom," I called. "Where. Is. James."

"Ah, oh yeah, sorry, hun, I can't focus properly in the presence of poly cotton. Maybe I'll donate some proper bedsheets to this hospital—"

"Tom!"

"Ugh, fine. He's with Wren at the station giving his statement. He'll be here in a bit. In the meantime, me and you need to have a little conversation."

Tom fixed the handkerchief he had poking out of his suit pocket as he spoke and then he looked at me.

"Soooooo, you and the sexy bodyguard, hey? Not bad for a first-timer, honey. You did good."

I laughed. "Thanks."

"Oh no, you're not having it that easy. Uncle Tom needs to know *all* the details. How big is he? Does he take his gun to bed? And by his gun I don't mean—"

I raised my hand. "Stop, stop, you're making me laugh, and it makes my head hurt."

"Anyway, now that you're gay we need to review your wardrobe. Oh wait, did it all burn in the fire?" He put his hand over his mouth and gasped. "I'm sorry, I didn't mean..."

"That's okay, Tom, I know what you meant. First of all, I

don't know what I am. I'll need to speak to James about it first, if that's okay. And second, I'll give you three outfit options," I said.

"Five."

"Four."

"Sold."

Tom clapped his hands and started looking me up and down as if he was already sizing me up for a fitting.

"Hey, can you take your eyes off my boyfriend and go pay attention to yours?"

I turned my head so fast toward the door of my room that my vision was momentarily blurry.

"Gladly," Tom said standing up. "It's been at least three hours since I've climbed him, and he's overdue for some attention."

"Thank you for the visual," James said, walking into the room and giving Tom a hug before coming over to the bed.

"Boyfriend, hey?" I said, holding his hand and pulling him down for a kiss.

"You did say you loved me, so I'm afraid you can't take it back."

I shook my head and smiled.

James sat on the bed and held my hands, rubbing circles with his thumbs.

"Did you really mean it, though? God, Connor, I'm so in love with you. I thought I was going to die when I saw you tied up in that cave."

My mouth was suddenly very dry. I'd blacked out after I'd made my declaration, so I didn't know if he ever said it back.

"I do, I love you. And I have no idea if that makes me gay, bisexual, or Jamessexual, but I don't care. As long as I'm with you, I know my heart is home."

He kissed me gently, not that it mattered because my body reacted all the same.

"Jamessexual. I like it. I love you, too, baby, so much," he said, smiling into my lips.

"Besides, you'll have a job getting rid of Bubbles. I think she and Donnie have got a little something going on."

"I think you're right," he said.

I stifled a yawn. "Will you be here when I wake up?" I asked.

"Scoot up," he asked and then laid next to me on the small bed. I turned to face him, burrowing against his chest. Until the bed broke down under our combined weight, I was going to enjoy this.

The hand running up and down my back was so soothing, I almost didn't want to wake up from my sleep.

"Hmm, don't stop," I said.

James's chest moved with his laughter under my head. "You don't have to wake up, you know."

"Need to pee," I said.

He helped me to the bathroom and then we settled on the bed again.

"The doctor came earlier when you were asleep. They said to call when you woke up so you can be discharged," he said.

"James, um...how are we going to do this?" I asked. Now that my mind had rested, I started to worry.

"Do what?"

"Us... You work for Kris, and you're away all the time. I don't have a place to live. Is this too complicated?" I asked, hating the doubt that was creeping in.

James cradled my face and tilted my head up so I could face him.

"Baby, this is the simplest my life has been since I was fifteen. Thanks to your brilliant idea and Mary's interfering nature, it seems I'm going into business with my siblings, which reminds me. I'm going to need to introduce you to them *and* I'm definitely borrowing my brother's car again."

I was so shocked that I couldn't even pick a part of his statement to ask more questions.

"Wait...rewind...you made up with your brother and sister?"

"We're working on it. They came back this morning, and I

was just so tired of arguing with them. Suddenly, your idea about the house and events came to me. I'm not a business person, but I know they both are, so I made them an offer."

I put my arms around his wide chest and breathed in his aftershave. "That is great. I'm so happy for you, baby. Having siblings is the worst, but it's also the best. Does this mean you're going to quit working for Charlie and Kris?"

"Not immediately. I won't leave them until after Aleks's wedding, but I was hoping you'd take over setting up the business with Eliza and Archie until I can come back here for good."

"Oh my god, are you serious? That would be amazing. I had so many ideas I wanted to run past you, but I didn't know if you'd be interested."

Until the nurse came in to discharge me, I ran through the list of ideas I had in my head for the house. James had to take out his phone, and he patiently typed everything in so we wouldn't forget.

A burst of energy zinged through me. This is what I loved doing and was good at. No more having to do someone's dirty work and fire hard-working people whenever they became too costly only to replace them with cheaper labor.

"Come on, baby," James said as soon as the nurse left. "Let's go home."

"Let's go. After all, I believe you made me a promise, and I'm hoping to collect," I teased, and he laughed.

We hadn't even left the car and Mary was already running over to fuss over me. Once I promised her I was fine and just needed a good night's sleep, she left us for the kitchen, saying something about making sure I was well-fed and strong as an ox.

James's brother and sister had left, too, but said they'd be back soon to discuss the proposal, so as soon as I checked in on my fickle turtle, who now couldn't care less about me, I pulled James up to the bedroom, bypassing the bed and going straight for the shower.

"I know I have an ugly bruise on my face, but I'm okay. In

fact, I've never felt better," I said, working James's clothes off of him before getting rid of mine. "So this is how it's going to go. We're going to get cleaned up so you can take me to bed and make me all hot and sweaty again."

James crashed his mouth onto mine, and I took the opportunity to get us close enough together that I could take both our hard cocks in hand.

He hissed as I teased his slit but still managed to reach out for the handle to turn the water in the shower on.

"I love your plan, baby, but you might need to be gentle with me today because my ass is still sore from last night," he said.

I pushed him under the water spray until he hit the tiled wall at the back, and before I went down on my knees for my man, I said, "That's okay, because I want you to make love to me tonight."

His cock hardened even more under my touch, and I couldn't wait to feel it inside of me.

JAMES

6 months later

"**B**ubbles!"

Hearing someone calling out for our little escape artist was a daily occurrence, but today I'd heard it at least a dozen times *and* from different people.

"She's here," I called out and then turned to the guilty pair. "Bubbles, Donnie, we need to have some rules in this house, okay? You guys can't go on a walkabout any time you want. And you, Donnie, you're such an enabler. Don't let her walk all over you."

A laugh came from the bedroom door. "It's exactly because she walks all over him that they keep going missing. Come on, Donnie, go take her back to her tank."

Donnie whimpered but got up and left the room with Bubbles laying on his back and holding on to his fur using her beak. I went to the door and saw the mutt go into the room where Bubbles' new, bigger tank was.

"We have some weird pets, right?" Connor asked as he crossed the room to wrap his arms around me and reach out for a kiss.

"Weird doesn't begin to define it, but at least they're obedient when they get caught. I bet Bubbles is already in the tank swimming while Donnie watches over her," I said.

"Anyway," he said, kissing my neck and pulling me closer against him. "You called for me?"

"Hmm...huh?" I moaned, my brain short-circuiting when Connor put his hands under my shirt and his fingers began to play with my nipples. Since he'd discovered how sensitive I was there, he used every opportunity to drive me crazy. "Fuck, baby...wait, wait, stop."

I pulled away and then laughed when I saw his pouting lips. Despite his height and size, especially since we'd started working out together, he looked adorable when he pouted.

"Come on," I pulled him by his hand, hoping to avoid the dozens of people that were busy hosting our first event.

"This is fabulous, darling. Well done! This is going to be the baby shower of the century," I heard Tom say to Amy, his assistant as they walked past us. I only had time to push Connor against a nearby column so we weren't seen.

"What's going on?" he asked, whispering.

"I'm trying to kidnap you, if that's okay. Do you know how many hours it's taken just to get you out of the house?" I whispered back.

"You realize this is a big day for us, James," he said.

"You have no idea..." I sighed.

"What do you mean?"

"Nothing. I need to take you somewhere before everyone gets here."

Connor poked his head around the column and said, "Okay, let's assess the situation. Mary is in the kitchen, Rupert is cutting up wood for the fire, and Tom and Amy are busy being Tom and Amy. We have a clear route to Archie's car."

I raised my hand with the keys, and Connor beamed.

"Let's go!" I said and took off running toward the car.

I started the car just in time to see Tom come round the corner with a roll of rainbow-colored fabric.

"We're going to be in trouble with Tom," Connor said. "He has his hands on his hips."

I laughed. "In that case, let's make this the greatest escape of all time."

The last six months had been such a rollercoaster. It was hard at first to be away from Connor when I had to return to Lydovia. I'd wanted to send Ryan to Windsor to keep an eye on my family, but everyone ganged up on me, so I was outnumbered.

Despite the distance, setting up a business together brought me closer to Archie and Eliza. For once, it didn't feel important to look back into the past. Those that were to blame were no longer with us, and the future felt brighter and full of potential. With Connor at my side, I knew I'd always be pulled in the right direction.

"What's worrying you?" I asked when I noticed him wringing his hands on his lap.

"Ellie."

"Is she okay? Have you had any news?"

"No, nothing."

Shortly after Connor's family came back from Lydovia after Brad was caught, we found out Ellie was pregnant. Hannah and Ellie had kept it a secret, but Ellie's best friend Ben, the owner of Bookmarked, had offered to be a sperm donor. Apparently, they'd agreed that once Ellie and Hannah had their baby, Ellie would then be a surrogate for Ben and Tristan.

So now, here we were, after months of hard work to get the house ready to host events, our first one was Ellie and Hannah's baby shower.

The whole Williams family seemed on the verge of a breakdown as if no woman ever had had a child before, and Ellie, bless her, was trying to hold it together.

The person that had surprised me the most, not surprisingly, was Connor. I'd been with him when he quit his job. Seeing Connor take charge was the hottest thing ever. Needless to say, we'd spent quite some time in bed after that particular phone call.

"Where are you taking us? Why are we in Chester Falls?" Connor asked.

I parked by the library and went around the other side of the car to meet Connor.

"Come with me," I said, holding out my hand.

It was a cold November day, but I'd been planning for this for months, and even if it snowed, I would stick to the original plan.

"Oh my god, is that an ice cream van?" Connor asked as we turned from the library onto the adjacent gardens.

"Yes, let's have one," I said.

"You're insane. It's freezing cold."

I wrapped my arms around Connor and made sure both the zipper of his coat and his scarf were all done up, and then I gave him a kiss that I knew would make his toes curl.

"Warm yet?" I teased.

"Fuck, give me the ice cream," he demanded.

When we got to the ice cream truck, we were handed a cup each with two scoops, one chocolate and peanut butter, and one vanilla.

Connor looked at me like I'd grown a second head.

"What's going on? How come you have a flavored ice cream? How come the truck is now closing? And you didn't pay for it."

Oh, I had paid, and quite handsomely. Who knew it was so hard to get hold of an ice cream truck during the winter months?

I put my hand on his lower back and guided him to the bench we used to sit at. When we got there, he stopped and turned to me.

"This is our bench," he said after he licked his spoon.

I placed both ice creams on the seat and took Connor's hands in mine. I didn't know if he already knew what I was going to do because his eyes were so shiny. It had to be more than just the cool breeze. It didn't matter. I was still going to say what I had to say.

"Connor, once upon a time I was a silly boy who thought he knew everything. Vanilla ice cream was the best. Always. And my best friend was the highlight of my days. Life has taken us in different directions, and somehow, we still ended up in the same place, with each other. Vanilla is no longer the best flavor, because thanks to you, I've opened my mind and my heart to try new things."

A small tear ran down his cheek. I removed my gloves and cleaned it up with my thumb, leaving my warm hands cradling his face.

"Connor Williams, you have always been my best friend, even when we weren't together. Your smile carried me through night after night during long deployments. It is now the highlight of my day, and I promise to make you smile for the rest of our lives if you give me the honor of being my husband."

More tears ran down his face as he nodded fiercely.

"Yes...yes, James. Nothing would make me happier than marrying you."

I pulled the box with the two rings from my pocket and put mine on before I removed his glove to put the other ring on his finger.

We hugged and kissed in the middle of the park for the longest time.

"Shall we go back home?" I asked.

"Um...can we keep this between us? I don't want to upstage Hannah and Ellie's baby shower," he said.

"Absolutely. Have you been around Tom this week? He might have kittens if he finds out we're engaged and haven't told him." I shuddered at my own words.

"Have you told Kris?" Connor asked.

"Yes, he's going to be my best man," I said, proud of my organizational skills.

"Then he's told Charlie, and Charlie already told Tom."

"Shit," I said.

I knew Tom would keep it a secret from the two moms to be,

but I was already dreading the onslaught of questions about the wedding.

"Baby..." Connor said, putting his arm around my waist as we walked back to the car.

"Yes?"

"Could we have Bubbles as our ring bearer?"

I laughed out loud at the image of Donnie walking down the aisle with Bubbles on his back, who in turn would have a little pillow with two rings on top of her carapace.

"Anything you want, baby."

Thank you so much for reading *How to Catch a Bodyguard*, the third book in the Chester Falls series. Keep reading to get a special bonus scene.

We've been dying to find out what really was going on with Connor since we met him in How to Catch a Prince, and what was behind the strange standoff with James at the end. I hope you've enjoyed finally figuring these two men out and boy what a story they have!

Up next is *How to Catch a Bachelor*. The cute baker from Spilled Beans is about to get into a blissfully wedded mess with the most conformed bachelor that has ever bachelored.

Be sure to follow me on Bookbub to be notified of new releases, and look for me on Facebook for sneak peaks of upcoming stories.

Please take a moment to write a review of *How to Catch a Bodyguard*. If you leave a review Connor will arrange for a one to one introduction to Bubbles- minus biting. For real!

If you would like to be the first to know when my new releases are available, read exclusive FREE stories and know what I'm up to, please sign up for my newsletter, Ana's VIP Readers: *bit.ly/AnaAshley*.

For giveaways, sneak peaks, ARC opportunities and general caffeinated fun times, please join my facebook group! Café RoMMance - Ana's Reader Group.

CELEBRATING THE ENGAGEMENT

CONNOR

I faceplanted on the bed with a groan.

As much as I loved my family, I was glad they'd left. Well, apart from Ellie and Hannah, who were staying the night in one of our new luxury rooms on the other side of the house.

The baby shower had been a resounding success, from the food to the decorations and all the little touches. Eliza and I had spent a long time on it, and we'd wanted it to be perfect.

I smiled when the bed dipped on my side and a strong, warm hand ran from my neck down to my ass, massaging each side and causing my dick to react instantly.

"If that's the back massage you promised me earlier, we need to have an anatomy lesson first," I said, my voice muffled by the bedcovers.

"I'm good at anatomy," James said with a soft chuckle before kissing the back of my neck, a spot he knew always drove me insane because I was so sensitive there.

"Hmmm..." was all I could manage as he continued before he turned me on my side so I could face him.

"Oh, there you are, fiancé," he said, placing his hand on my cheek and leaning over to kiss me. It was a gentle kiss, but there was so much love and reverence in how his lips touched mine that I almost choked with emotion.

"Today went well, right?" I asked, a little doubt creeping in.

"Hands down the best day of my life," he said, leaning his head on his elbow and taking my hand in his, kissing the finger that now wore my engagement band.

"That's not what I meant," I said, pulling him down for another kiss. "Everyone liked the baby shower, didn't they?"

"Were you there, sweetheart? They loved every second."

"But how about when—"

He cut me off with a searing kiss that made me forget about the baby shower and wonder why we weren't naked yet.

"My answer won't change," he said. "The house could have burned down, and today would still be the best day of my life."

My heart swelled as I remembered his proposal earlier today. All my life, I always assumed I'd be the one to propose to someone, but James had done something truly special by making it about us and our shared history.

He'd been so right. We'd never stopped being best friends because even though I'd become close to Rory after James left, our friendship had never quite been the same.

There was something more guarded about Rory that I could never penetrate completely, and I'd missed the openness of James, his sweet innocence, and how he just seemed to get me.

"What are you thinking about?" he asked, running his thumb over my lower lip. I took it in my mouth and sucked, showing him how I'd take care of another part of his anatomy. His eyes went impossibly dark with lust.

"I was thinking about your proposal and how we were always destined to be together," I said after releasing his finger with a pop.

"I did good, didn't I?" he asked with the cockiest grin I'd ever seen.

"Meh." I shrugged.

He punched my shoulder, and I took the opportunity to pull him closer until he was on top of me. God, how I relished his weight pinning me down.

"What do you say about that anatomy class?" I asked.

James took my hands and restrained them over my head. His hard cock pressed against mine and his undulating hips put me in danger of coming sooner than I wanted.

Tonight was special. Our first night together as fiancés. The first night of a new chapter in our lives. And now that James was back in Windsor for good, there was a lot to celebrate.

"Will you help me with that anatomy lesson?" he asked, crashing his mouth onto mine.

I wiggled my way out from under him and got out of bed. "Come on, practice makes perfect," I said, walking backward away from the bed and unbuttoning my shirt slowly until I reached the bottom and untucked it.

James got up like his ass was on fire and was undressed even before I'd reached for the zipper on my slacks.

I laughed. "So much for my seduction plan."

"Baby," he said, in a deep voice, advancing toward me. "First, I found you facedown on our bed like you were ready to drop. And second," he said, coming so close we were nearly touching but not quite, "you seduce me every day as soon as I wake up and look into those gorgeous green eyes, your hair that won't make up its mind if it's going to be red or brown, and especially those cute freckles that are like stars lighting my path into your heart."

My throat tightened. "What did I do to deserve you?" I asked, shaking my head as I stared into his hazel eyes.

"You exist, Connor. That's all."

He removed my slacks because my hands were too shaky.

"Come on, baby, let's get in the shower. I plan on cleaning you before I make you dirty and then repeat it all over again," he said.

I sighed happily and followed the love of my life into the

bathroom, admiring the beautiful curves of his body. My gangly Jamie Lexington had grown into a sex-on-legs, magazine-model-worthy adult, and I still hadn't decided whether my favorite part of him was the two dimples on his lower back just above his delicious bubble butt or the *V* running down from his abs toward that long, thick cock I loved so much.

"My eyes are up here, baby," he said, smirking as he turned on the shower.

"Eye contact is overrated," I said, making a show of my appreciation of his body.

I stepped forward and ran my hands all over his back, feeling the result of all the hard work he put in at the gym and around the house. I kissed the three little scars on his shoulder where the bullets that ended his military career had hit him.

He'd been in war zones risking his life for our country. I was so proud of him, but whenever I saw those scars, I also saw the possibility that he may have never returned and found me again. Then again, it was thanks to those scars that he'd been able to come back. It was a love-hate relationship that I kept to myself because there was no point worrying about something in the past. We had a bright and happy future ahead of us.

As soon as James was satisfied the water was at the right temperature, he walked into the shower, taking me with him.

Our mouths clashed in a messy dance of tongues and water that left us breathless and giggly.

"Why are shower-kissing scenes so sexy, but then you do it in real life and nearly drown?" James asked, reaching for the soap and lathering it in his hands.

Our erections occasionally rubbed as we took turns washing each other, but when I tried to take them in my hand, he slapped it away.

"I've got plans for those," James said, turning me to face the glass shower wall. The new position meant the water wasn't running over my head, so he turned my head around to face him, and keeping one hand on my neck, he kissed me, his tongue seeking entry into my mouth. He tasted like strawberry, likely because of one of Tom's nonalcoholic cocktails he'd had earlier.

"Hmmm, you taste delicious," I moaned against his lips, feeling him smile against mine.

He placed my hands on the glass, giving me a heated look that told me to keep them there before he went down on his knees.

I obeyed, knowing it would end well for me.

He chuckled as I arched my back to give him better access.

"Someone's eager," he said, but I didn't have a chance to reply before he ran his tongue from my perineum to my hole, paying it the same attention as he did my mouth earlier.

"Fuuuck, baby, that feels so good..." I moaned.

"Hmm, I think you taste better than I do," he said and then returned to teasing my hole. My cock leaked like crazy, and he hadn't even added any fingers.

He got up and aligned his body with mine, pushing me into the glass and brushing his cock over my crease. My body lit up every time he teased my hole with his crown. I knew he wouldn't push in without lube, but the promise of it had all my cylinders firing. James knew all too well how much I loved the feeling of that first stretch, and boy did he take advantage of it every time he could.

If someone had told me a year ago how much I'd love bottoming, and for none other than a man, I'd have laughed my head off.

"Tell me how much you want me inside you, baby," he whispered into my ear.

"More than ice cream," I said all too quickly, making him chuckle.

He kept his teasing pace and then wrapped his hand around my cock, stroking it in sync with the movement of his hips.

"Knowing how much you love ice cream, I think I better hurry then. In fact, I think we should add some ice cream to this party," he said, licking a path from my shoulder to my earlobe and then sucking on it.

"Don't you dare fucking stop, James Bennett. There's a reason we have a bottle of lube in the shower. Use it. Now!" I demanded.

He groaned and released my cock. "Fuck, baby, I love it when you take charge. Seeing you this desperate to have my cock inside you."

I was going to tell him to stop with the dirty talk and get to the dirty business when a lubed finger pushed through the tight ring of muscles.

"Ungh..." I moaned. "God, it feels so good. More, James...more."

"Shh, baby, I'll give you everything you need."

A second finger joined the first, and by the time he added a third, I was threatening divorce if he didn't put his cock in me, and we weren't even married yet.

"I get so hard when you're like this, Connor. I won't last when I'm inside you," he said.

"And you think I will with the way you've been teasing me?"

My laugh got stuck in my throat and my breath caught when I felt the head of James's cock seeking permission to enter. I relaxed and stood still to allow him time to get all the way in. As much as I loved that initial breach, pain wasn't my kink, so I was glad he took his time working his cock in.

"So fucking tight," he gasped. "So perfect."

"Please, James..." I had no idea what I was begging for, but he seemed to know because he started with slow thrusts that changed into longer ones as my channel adjusted to his size. Yep, my husband-to-be was a big boy, and I loved every inch of him.

I didn't even realize the water was running cold because all I felt inside was scorching heat.

My orgasm built in the bottom of my spine, and I knew it wouldn't take long for me to go over.

"James!" I cried.

The beauty of being with someone who knew you better than yourself was that sometimes words were redundant because they knew exactly what you were asking for. In James's case, I wanted the pleasure-pain of the fast and sharp thrusts that set my insides on fire every time his cock hit my prostate.

I was like the Vitruvian man, legs open wide, arms stretched out, and my cock painfully hard against the glass as James got so deep inside me that his balls hit mine with every move.

"So close," he said in my ear.

"I want to feel you come inside me first," I said, hoping I'd be able to keep my orgasm at bay long enough.

"Connor!" he shouted, his orgasm filling me with his warm release.

I finally allowed myself to move my arms, placing them on his hips as a silent request for him to stay inside a little longer.

He turned my head and kissed me with such fierce passion. His cock finally slipped out, leaving me feeling empty but still in need of release.

I turned around and pushed him back down on his knees.

"Lesson's not over," I said.

He took my cock in his mouth and sucked it straight to the back of his throat. A few thrusts into his mouth, and I was coming so hard I thought I would pass out.

I held myself upright until my legs felt like jelly and I slid to the floor where James already sat with a blissful expression.

"You definitely taste better," he said.

We stayed there until the goosebumps on my skin gave away how cold I was.

"Come on, let's warm you up in bed," James said.

He picked up two towels that had been warming on the radiator, and we dried ourselves before going back into the room. I was glad we'd added a few more logs to the fire earlier.

The first thing I saw as I stepped back into the bedroom was the door wide open. The second thing was Donnie lying by the fire with Bubbles happily sleeping on his back.

James groaned, "We have weird fucking pets."

"We will never live this down," I said, closing the bedroom

door and hoping Ellie's pregnancy was making her and Hannah tired enough that they were sleeping and hadn't heard us.

"Come on, Mr. Williams, let's get you cozy in bed. If you're lucky, I might let you make out with me," he said, taking my hand and leading me toward the bed.

"How about future Mr. Bennett?" I teased.

He scrunched his nose and shook his head.

"Mr. Lexington-Bennett?" I tried again, referring to him changing his last name months ago when he'd accepted both his father's and mother's surnames.

I pulled the covers up and snuggled against his chest. It was my absolute favorite place to be.

"How about Mr. Williams?" he said.

"I'm already Mr. Williams," I said, stifling a yawn.

"What if I want to be Mr. Williams too?" he said.

I stared into his eyes and thought about how lucky I was to be right where I belonged. For the first time in my life, everything made sense, and if I could talk to the Connor of eighteen months ago, I would tell him he wasn't lost or unlovable. He just needed a new home.

"That sounds perfect."

PREVIEW OF HOW TO CATCH A BACHELOR

INDY

The doorbell dinged. It was already way past closing time, and, as usual, I'd gotten too distracted following my closing routine to lock the door to my coffee shop or even flip the closed sign for that matter.

Not that it would make a difference, because as long as I was out front, there was nothing that would keep my love-sick customers away.

"Hey, Maggie, how's it going?" I asked, not bothering to turn around from where I was behind the counter cleaning the coffee machine. Maggie had come in after-hours every day for the last week suffering from a severe case of seemingly unrequited love. I wasn't so sure it was unrequited but more that the object of her affection was oblivious to her interest.

I heard a deep sigh and plastered the most sympathetic smile I could manage at this time of day before turning around.

"Liam doesn't even know I exist," she said, crossing her arms and pouting.

"Did you speak to him like I suggested?"

Maggie blushed and uncrossed her arms, looking down at the floor.

"Ugh, I'm such a loser. He came in the store and asked if I

could fix his rod. I thought he was flirting with me, so I said yes, I'd fix his rod any time. Then he went back to his car and brought out his fishing rod. I literally died."

I had to bite the inside of my cheek so I wouldn't laugh at poor Maggie or point out that since she worked at the fish and tackle shop, Liam's question hadn't been totally out of place.

"So did you, erm...fix his rod?"

"Yes, of course I did." She looked at me like it was the strangest thing to doubt her rod mending abilities.

"Aaand?"

"And then he left."

"Did you make any polite chat or ask him questions?" I asked.

"I tried, but he only answered with yes and no, so after a while I gave up. I know I need to move on from this crush, but I really like him, Indy. The other day I saw him help little Mikey when the chain on his bike came loose. I *literally* melted watching him. He's older, more experienced, and probably would never look at someone like me, but my stupid heart won't stop lusting after him."

She fell on one of the chairs as if she'd lost all hope.

"Oh, Mags." I went around the counter and crouched by her knees, taking her hands in mine. "I don't know Liam very well, but I know what it's like to try to move on after you lose someone. If he's not taking your hints, why don't you try asking him out for a coffee?"

She looked at me with her big blue eyes, a tiny sliver of hope dancing across her pupils.

"What if he says no?" she asked, her voice so little my heart broke for her.

"But what if he says yes?"

Maggie seemed to think about it and made some kind of resolution in her mind. She got up and gave me a hug before leaving.

I took the opportunity to flip the sign to closed and turn the lock on the door, but at that same moment, I saw my friend Ben, the owner of Bookmarked, the only bookstore in Chester Falls, run across the square waving his hand.

"Hey, Indy," he said, out of breath. "Oh jeez, I need to start going to the gym. I'm so out of shape."

"You're saying Tristan doesn't give you good workouts?" I teased.

"Oh, stop it. Not you, too."

I laughed. It was a running joke among our group of friends that whenever Ben and Tristan were in the storeroom at Bookmarked, they were making out because that's how they'd gotten together in the first place.

"How can I help? I know you're not coming to me at this hour for love problems."

He shook his head. "Nope, all good in the love department. In fact, I have some news." Ben paused, his eyes twinkling with happiness.

"Oh my god, he's proposed, hasn't he?" I said, clapping my hands together over my chest.

Ben nodded, and I squealed. I mean, there is only one possible reaction when two of your good friends decide to get married. Squeal. All. The. Way.

"Congratulations. I'm so happy for you two. Have you set a date? I doubt Tristan will want a long engagement."

I gestured for Ben to follow me inside and went around the counter to box up a few cinnamon buns I had left over for him to take home.

"He'd happily go down to the courthouse tomorrow, but he wouldn't dare upset my mom just in case she stops making him his favorite peach cobbler," Ben said.

"Can't blame him. I tried to pry the recipe from her last week, and even after I gave her a box of cupcakes, she still didn't budge."

"That's my mom for you. Anyway, I came over to ask if you'd like to join us for brunch on Sunday at Benny's," he said. "There's some wedding stuff we'd like to run by you."

"Momma Ruth's blueberry pancakes and wedding talk? Wouldn't miss it for the world."

Ben smiled and then beamed as I gave him the box with his favorite treats.

"My wedding diet will now start tomorrow because Tristan is working late tonight and these babies are going to keep me company," he said, raising the box up to his face, inhaling deeply and rolling his eyes like he'd just taken a hit of his favorite drug.

"Your secret is safe with me," I said with a chuckle, watching as he walked back to Bookmarked. There was a lightness to him since he'd met Tristan, and I couldn't be happier for both of them.

My phone rang just as I locked up and made the short walk up the stairs outside the building to my apartment. Living above my business meant I had to make an extra effort to go out and exercise or walk on my days off, but after closing Spilled Beans, I couldn't deny it was handy not having a commute.

"Hey, Mom, how's it going," I said, toeing my shoes off by the door and answering the call.

"Hi, honey. I'm good, but my fridge is decidedly empty, and I'm definitely not on a diet."

"I will never understand why on earth you'd keep cake inside the fridge."

"Because I like it cold. Besides, it doesn't matter, anyway, because I haven't got any cake, do I?"

I chuckled.

"How about I visit tomorrow and bring you a freshly made one?"

"I would just be happy to see you, honey. You know that."

"Yes, but you'll be happier if I don't turn up empty-handed. Don't pretend that's not the reason you called."

She let out an outraged gasp. "You know me so well. Your dad sends his love."

"Fine, I'll make him a tray of blondies, too."

"Good. I'll make sure to have a pot of your favorite coffee brewing. It's been a while since I grilled you over your love life."

"Mom," I groaned.

"What? A mother can't be interested in her son's happiness?"

"I'm fine, and there's no love life to talk about, so that'll be a very short discussion." I laughed to mask the sudden sinking feeling in the pit of my stomach.

"Indigo, honey, you're not going to wake up married one day."

"I know," I said before we said our goodbyes and ended the call.

I sank into my sofa and looked at the clock on the wall. It was only nine o'clock. For most people, this was the time they were relaxing in front of the TV with a drink or maybe even dinner.

For me, this was bedtime. I was up most days at four to start baking in time to open Spilled Beans with all the fresh treats my customers were now used to.

My schedule and relationships weren't ingredients that went together in the same recipe. I'd slowly come to that realization after all the times I'd started seeing someone regularly only to be dumped when I couldn't have a movie night without falling asleep, go out dancing, or do anything that required being conscious past ten at night.

"Stop it, Indy. No one likes a party pooper. It's the weekend, and for once, you're off work, so dust off the self-pity," I said to myself.

My phone dinged with a message, but what caught my eye as I unlocked the screen was the hookup app that had laid dormant for longer than I cared to remember.

The last message I'd exchanged with someone had a January date stamp. Fuck, had it really been four months since I last got laid? No wonder I was feeling funky.

I removed the elastic band from my hair, leaving it to fall in long waves over my shoulders, and massaged my scalp.

Most of my friends were now all loved up, and as much as I

loved seeing them so happy, there was a part of me that was jealous. I also wanted to come home after a long day on my feet to cuddle up to a hard chest and strong arms.

My dick twitched at the thought, so I decided to put it out of its misery and see if there was anyone interesting around.

I scrolled past some of the local guys who were online because I wasn't in the mood for a catch-up. As much as the familiarity of hooking up with someone I already knew was comfortable, tonight, I could do with hard, fast, and anonymous.

"Well, hello, Mr. Washboard Abs. Let me grab my laundry, and I'll be right with you," I said to myself before sending the guy a message and jumping in the shower. Hopefully, soon enough I'd get dirty again.

CONNECT WITH ANA

Connect with Ana on social media:

Hang out in my FB Group:
facebook.com/groups/CafeRoMMance
Follow me on instagram: *instagram.com/anawritesmm/*
Follow me on Bookbub: *bookbub.com/authors/ana-ashley*
Sign up to my newsletter: *bit.ly/AnaAshley*

For an overview of all of Ana's books and audiobooks, visit her website: *anawritesmm.com/books*

BOOKS BY ANA ASHLEY

Single Dads of Stillwater
A spin off series from Chester Falls that can be read on its own. Each book features one or more single dads in this community of friends, family and found family. In this contemporary MM romance series you'll find heat, emotion and a guaranteed happy ever after.
Newcomer
Antagonist
Breakthrough
Heartstring
Datebook (Coming early 2024)

Finding You Series
A standalone series set across the Atlantic between New York and Portugal. Find your way home with this contemporary MM romance series with friends to lovers, star-crossed lovers and age gap with plenty of heat, feels and always a happy ever after.
Home Again
Together Again
Love Again
And for a special short story, Complete Again, plus bonus scenes, grab the Finding You boxset now.

Room for 3 series
This is a high heat MMM contemporary romance series set in an island resort.
The Resort
The Vacation (Free short story)

Chester Falls Series
From a Prince to a Happy Ever After for all, enjoy this small town MM romance series that's as sweet as they come, with plenty of heat, humor and everything in between.
How to Catch a Bookworm (Prequel short)
How to Catch a Prince
How to Catch a Rival
How to Catch a Bodyguard
How to Catch a Bachelor

How to Catch the Boss (a Christmas novella)
How to Catch a Biker
How to Catch a Vet
How to Catch a Happy Ever After
You can now have all the books in the series and the prequel all in two boxsets.
Chester Falls Collection Volume I
Chester Falls Collection Volume II

Standalone books
Christmas Bubble: a low angst, standalone, Christmas novel featuring a petite but larger-than-life cheerleader, an older demisexual football coach and a winter cabin by the lake with only one bed. With cameos from Chester Falls and Stillwater.
Midnight Ash: a sweet Cinderella fairytale retelling with a sexy kinky twist on the side, and a cast who don't quite behave as you'd expect.
Stronghold: a sweet and sexy romance in Sarina Bowen's World of True North, Vino & Veritas series. This is a standalone story between two child-hood friends who reunite after as decade apart, with some creative use of maple syrup.

FREE READS
My Fake Billionaire
The Vacation

ABOUT ANA

Ana Ashley was born in Portugal but has lived in the United Kingdom for so long, even her friends sometimes doubt if she really is Portuguese.

After getting hooked on reading gay romance, Ana decided to follow her lifelong dream of becoming an author.

These days you can find her in front of her laptop bringing her stories to life, or in the kitchen perfecting her recipe for the famous Portuguese custard tarts.

Ana Ashley writes sweet and steamy gay romance set in America, often in small towns where everyone knows everyone.

You can follow Ana on the usual social media hangouts.

For access to exclusive teasers, content, and general book and food related goodness you can now join Ana in her Facebook Group, Café RoMMance - Ana's Reader Group

Ana's VIP Readers - bit.ly/AnaAshley

Facebook Page - @anawritesmm

Email - ana@anaashley.com

Instagram - @anawritesmm

Bookbub - bookbub.com/authors/ana-ashley

Goodreads - goodreads.com/ana-ashley